KISS NUMBER 8

KISS NUMBER 1
SETH

KISS NUMBER 2
GREGORY

KISS NUMBER 5
KEVIN M.

KISS NUMBER 6
KEN'ICHI

KISS NUMBER 3
KEVIN S.

KISS NUMBER 4
JONATHAN

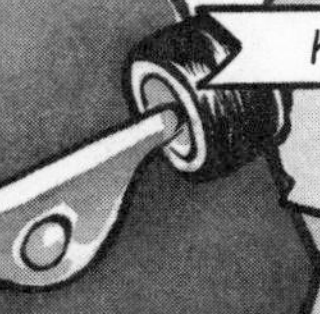

KISS NUMBER 7
ADAM

KISS
NUMBER
8

KISS NUMBER 8

WRITTEN BY
COLLEEN AF VENABLE

ARTWORK BY
ELLEN T. CRENSHAW

First Second
NEW YORK

2004
I've never understood the world's obsession with kissing.
BUSH CHENEY '04
And "swapping spit?" That's supposed to make me want to do it?

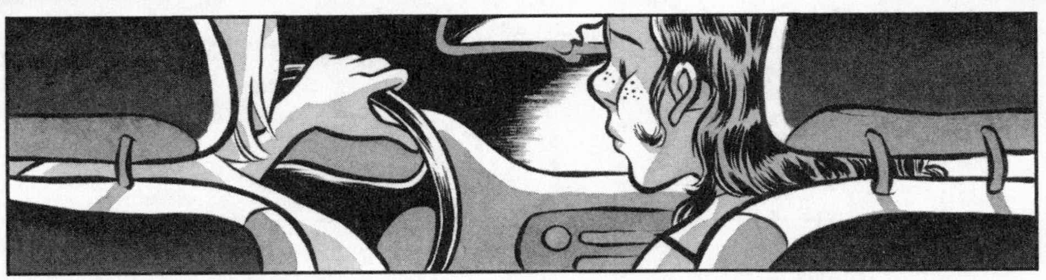

KISS NUMBER 1
I guess my first wasn't so bad.

Though I remember having no idea what to do with my arms.

KISS NUMBER 2
My best friend Cat told me I should hold his face gently. And close my eyes. Don't forget. Close my eyes. Close my eyes.

Whoa! Is that Rhode Island? How does a zit get that big?!

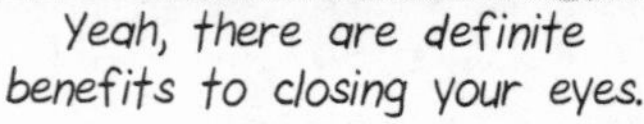
Yeah, there are definite benefits to closing your eyes.

Uh. I gotta go.

KISS NUMBER 3
Luckily, I wasn't afraid to use my arms by my third kiss.

I'll call you.

What the...
Pretty sure his tongue hit my small intestines, though he was kind enough to lick most of my face en route.

There were plenty after that.

All with varying degrees of "meh."

KISS NUMBER 4
This one guy always led into kisses teeth-first. Teeth against teeth: Worst sound in the world. Rattles through you from your head to your toenails.
CLANK!

KISS NUMBER 5
Gahh!
heh, heh
There was another boy. He would put his tongue between my front teeth and upper lip. He thought it was funny. I...
...did not agree.

KISS NUMBER 6
I don't quite remember all of them.

KISS NUMBER 7
I wish I didn't remember more.

But none came close to the awfulness that followed KISS NUMBER 8.

Laura, I didn't mean...
I SAID GET OUT! GET OUT!

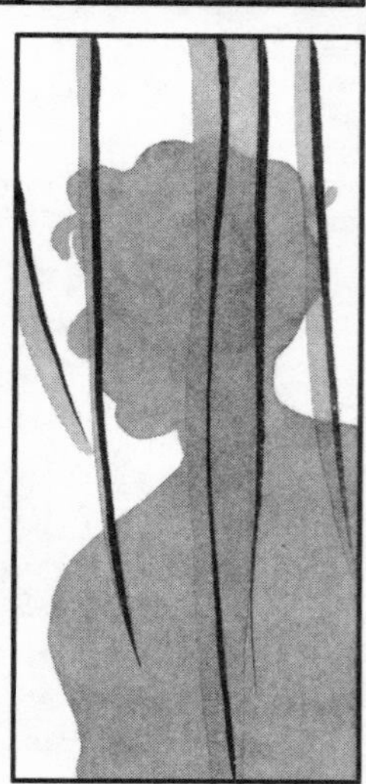

One month earlier.

You can't deny that he's totally hot.

You're going to hell, Cat. You know that, right?
Shhhh. My parents are gonna get pissed.

I mean, look at those abs!

Great, now Adam thinks we're talking about him.
Mmmf.

body, which is given up for you.
If we get more decent-looking altar boys, maybe I'll stop drooling over our lord and savior.

...given up for you?
Adam, bells.

So, you're telling me you come to church because you have the hots for Jesus?
Nooo. I have the hots for THAT SCULPTURE of Jesus.
Mom's gonna kill him.
Clang clang clang clang
Shhhh.

Shame you never get to see the back. Betcha Jesus's got an ass that could crack a walnut... Hell, I bet it could shell a cashew!
Ewwwww.

What are you up to?
Normal Sunday: Tornadoes game. You should come.

Uh. No. Who watches minor-league baseball? It's just a bunch of overweight old farts secretly hoping they strike out 'cause there is NO WAY they're gonna run with those beer babies.

What about you, Laura?
Well...

Maybe it'll be good to not be in my house for a bit.
Woo! Makeover! Amanda, say goodbye to Laura's forehead caterpillar.

Goodbye, Amanda. I shall miss you!
Stop that.

Hey, Mom and Pop Orham!

Mrs. Stevenson tells me she heard you girls use the Lord's name in vain... How many times was it?
I don't remember.

Eighteen!

Eighteen times?
We weren't using it in VAIN. I was praising him! And besides, it was only like thirteen—maybe fourteen times.
And I'll never eat a cashew again.

No idea what she's talking about.
Jim, stop encouraging them. Girls, we let you try it, but no more sitting together.

Dad! We didn't do anything wrong.
I'm sure Adam was flirting with someone else when he forgot to ring the bells.

Ew, he's like my brother.
Ew, he IS my brother.
Eh, he did have a decent growth spurt lately...

Whaat? Like you guys didn't notice!

Let's go. If we leave the Tornado crew for too long there won't be any food left.
Need a ride, Cat?

Never again!
Lord, help us all.
Nineteen!

Season Passes AVAILABLE!
TORNADOES STADIUM
One large cheese fries.
THIS WEEK'S TORNEATO GIFTS!!!
Who will win today's running
Tornadoes

CONCESSIONS
ORDER HERE
Cold Cola
You know, I think Adam can do better than Cat.
Cat and Adam? Gross. Way to put that picture in my head.

She's right, though. Adam really has grown up a lot recently.
Please don't tell me you're trying to fix me up with Adam!

Of course I'm not.
How much cheese?
Do you really have to ask?

So, if you aren't interested in Adam, is there somebody else I should know about?
Daaad.

It's been a while! You used to have a new boyfriend every week.

There was Kevin, Kevin, Kevlar—I think his parents mighta done some drugs...
John, Paul, George, Ringo, Shemp...

I'm just saying if you're dating someone in the witness protection program, I'm really good at keeping secrets.
I would only turn him in if the mob offered, like, twenty bucks or free cheese fries.
Dad, there're only forty guys at St. Francis and I'm pretty sure I already dated any worth trying out.
FIIIINE. I'll let you marry Franco. But I'm not super happy about the age difference.
Franco looks like he swallowed a basketball.
But you've got shared interests. You both want him to play in games. You always said you were going to marry him.
Yeah, in FIFTH GRADE. But I also really wanted to marry Leopardman from Danger Cats.
Ah, yes. Leopardman. How could I forget, right before Shemp.
I'd rather have my grandkids be Tornado fans than badly animated crime-fighting cats.
I demand a subject change. Superpower. Which one? Go!

I always said that Cat was my best friend, but that's not really true. My best friend position was filled long before I met her.
Really? You'd pick invisibility over flying?
It's more practical.
But flying! Imagine it! Also, you picked invisibility last time.

So? There's no rule against picking the same thing twice.
Get your asses down! You wanna jinx the whole first inning?

Relax! We've got time. Free Bird's still primping.

Hey, Mads.
Adam.

Didn't think you'd be here. Saw your mom biting your head off after mass.
Father Tim saved me, walks right up and says I'm one of the best altar boys he's ever had.
Geez, I hope that's not true.
And voilà, here I am. That Tim is headed for sainthood.
How's O'Callaghan looking?
No signs of the injury. We got this one.
Oh please, he always chokes. I don't care how much they paid for him. They should just start—
Franco.
You and your Franco. Ha.
He's ancient. Sure, he can pitch one or two good innings, but if he did a whole game we'd be signing "get well soon" on a stuffed bear's ass.
What are you doing?! Sit down!

Oh no. I think my arm's stuck.
I've never understood this one. I mean, we're gonna have to stand in like two seconds anyway.
Har. Har. Get down, Jim.

Listen, you're not SUPPOSED to stand until the Free Bird tells you. Totally jinxes the whole first inning.
And this has been proven how?
With science!

Lots of lab rats in uniforms, tiny bleachers, one rat in sequins and shoulder pads...
Took FOREVER to teach it the national anthem.

Don't be ridicul—

What the hell?
Leg cramp.

It's contagious!

Buncha idiots.

PLEASE RISE FOR THE SINGING OF OUR NATIONAL ANTHEM.

Don't blame me when O'Callaghan farts all over the mound.

Whose broad stripes and bright stars, thru' the perilous fight...

...ramparts we wa
Doo, doot, dooo, dooooo.

...that our flag was still there...
Doo, doot
dooo
dooooo

O'er the land of the...

FREE

PLAY BALL!
Wooo!
Yeah!
Woo!

All right, boys! Show 'em what you got!
Doesn't seem fair Mrs. Girsky never has to take off her hat.
You don't want to see that. Pretty sure her hair's attached.

You okay?
Booo!
What? Oh, yeah.

Just a client. Must not have known it was a home game.
Tell me he did not just hit the first batter.
Ohhh.

C'mon, O'Callaghan!
Doo, doot, dooo, dooooo.

See? What did I tell you? You joked about it, but here it is. Right here. SCIENCE.

THAT WAS A STRIKE!
This is painful. Mom shoulda grounded me.

Jesus, Jimmy! Tell your girlfriend to stop calling!
Bzzzzz. Bzzzzz.
Sorry. I should find out what's so urgent. Be right back.

Ball four!
Booo!
Oh, come on!

Crap! Sorry. Sorry.
Cheese!
Cheese?

Oh.
Cheese.

Franco better be pitching by the time I get back.

See, this is why I don't want to date Adam: dry-cleaning bills.
What the hell do you want, Dina? You're not supposed to call me.

Our relationship was over a long time ago. No, Amanda doesn't know. I'm raising her right. There's no room for you or...

I...I didn't know.

sigh
No. I'll be there. Two thirty. Saturday.

NCESSIONS

Oh geez, Mads. You're still soaked.
Let me guess—they wouldn't give you napkins without buying something. Girsky gets cheaper every year.

Um. No. Yeah. No, they were out.
I'll go get you some TP. It's a great excuse to stop watching this bloodbath you guys started.
We started?
Make fun of my superstitions, but you know I'm right this time.

Hmmm, so it rained cheese? I miss anything else?

Who was on the phone?

Just some client really desperate to sign the house on Elmore.
What client?

Hey, look, Mads! They're taking O'Callaghan out. This may be your lucky day.

FRANCO
40
MAR
11

TORN

TORN

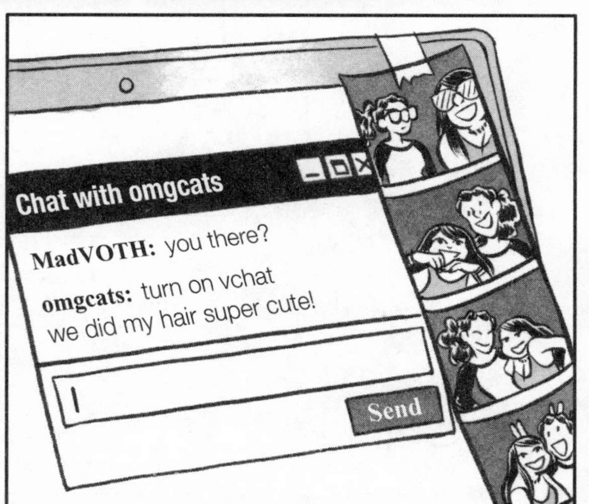

MadVOTH: can't mom-monster too close-by. pic?

omgcats: k!

picture loading...

MadVOTH: something weird happened today
omgcats: what did u actually meet a guy u didn't instantly hate? LOL
MadVOTH: shutup! just because one of us has standards!
omgcats: jk u know i luv u
BEST♡FRIEND
Chat with omgcats
MadVOTH: i think my dad had an affair
omgcats: gtfo! no way
MadVOTH: i heard him with some woman on the phone.
omgcats: that's crzy
your mom may be a bitch
but she's hot & he knows it
no way he's sleeping around
he's like a priest minus the tendency to touch lil boys
speaking of which srsly
Adam has a total hrd-on for u
swear i could see it through his robe
puberty is being nice 2 that boy
MadVOTH: maybe you're right, but it really sounded…
omgcats: shit mom's drunk ranting again brb

omgcats: [idle]
sigh

BING!
laurapage3: How was the game?
Ugh. Do you have to message me every time I'm online, Laura?

MadVOTH: game sucked
not a fun day for many reasons

laurapage3: Many reasons? What else happened?
By the way, I wanted to apologize for being so stressed this morning. Mom has been a royal pain lately.
MadVOTH: know the feeling can't believe adam didn't get in trouble!

Who're you talking to?
None of your business.

Amanda's asking about me?!
Stop reading over my shoulder.

Ask her if she'd go out with me!
Get rejected on your own time.
laurapage3: Actually, he's grounded all next weekend.

I am not! Dammit, Laura! Why would you do that?

BING!
MadVOTH: poor kid he seriously needs to find someone his age to crush on he's like an excitable puppy…one that spills drinks on me.

MadVOTH: soooo crazy story…

laurapage3: What?

MadVOTH: i think my dad's having an affair, or had an affair. like past tense.

laurapage3: Oh god. That's horrible!

MadVOTH: he said something like "their relationship was over" and then started to cry and he agreed to meet her next sat.

laurapage3: Holy crap. Are You Okay?

MadVOTH: i'm freaking out. what if it's another kid or something? what if they get back together?

laurapage3: Listen, I have to go. Adam has some project.
MadVOTH: oh. never mind. forget i said anything.

laurapage3: No! I want to hear the whole story. Let's talk about it tomorrow.
Hang in there! If you need me call.
MadVOTH: can't really talk out loud about this.
Laura...
I know, I know!

sigh

GIMMEG

There was no way my dad would have cheated. No way.

Hey, Amanda?
Yeah.
FRANCO

Shoes off the bed.

They aren't touching anything!
Then you can have fun washing the sheets.

FINE.
Watch your tone. You're lucky I'm not more upset about your behavior at mass.

I didn't do anything!
Well, now you will do something. Wash the sheets.

Who am I kidding? Dad could do better.
Get the futon cover, too.

VALLEY OF THE HIDDEN
You wouldn't put up with this crap, would you?

And before you know it you'd kill for a plain cube of tofu. KILL. It's like all you can think about. Bland, squishy, jiggly...

Enough, I get it.

I wouldn't want to eat her. Haha.

Not everyone cheats.
Say hi to Tweedle-Dum in Delusional Disneyland. Can you imagine what it would be like to only kiss one person forever?

BRRRRRRIIING
Crap.

Let's talk about something more fun, like...

The Spanish-American War?! Ohmigod, that was my favorite. How did you know, Ms. White?

WHAT'S UP, ALL YOU BREAKERS?! WELCOME TO HIT THE BREAKS. I'M YOUR HOST, MARIO RODRIGUEZ.
Two days of the week had a truly sacred schedule.
Sundays it was me, Dad, mass, and a Tornadoes game.
Tuesdays it was me, Dad, Jeopardy!, Valley of the Hidden, and Hit the Breaks.
But that day Dad didn't show. No call. Nothing.

bzzzzz

Cat
mario's nips are outta control! some dancer's gonna lose an eye!
Reply
Options

He's a robot.
Those aren't nipples.
They're wingnuts.

click

Hey.

What a horrible day.

Forget to get something?
Crap. The mail. Sorry.
Don't worry. I love working for you and your dad.

Also, for the record, "doing the wash" doesn't mean putting things in the machine and leaving them wet overnight.
Whoops.

You're lucky I'm too tired to yell. AC went out halfway through Pilates 3. Wanted to cancel, but level three'ers actually liked sweating more.

Anything for me?
Bill. Bill. Bill. 0 percent APR. Bill. Bill.

No. Nothing.
Gram and Gramp are slacking on cruise postcards.

Well, Alaska's a lot farther than the Keys.

What's that face for?

Tired. I'm just tired. Where's your dad?
Thought you could tell me.

I need a shower.

Hey, why don't we watch a movie together tonight?
One of your Lifetime ones? Yeah, think I'll pass.

Sorry to snap before. It's just been a rough day. I love you.
Love you, too.

click

Any breakers better than me yet?
Where've you been?

Heeey. Did you skip work and sneak off to the water park again? Not fair!

Haha. Very funny.
Sorry, Mads. Open house on Lennox went late. How was VOTH?
Don't know. Was waiting for you.

Actually, I was hoping we could all watch a movie together.
That's my girl! Cue it up.
Amanda, you pick.

If we don't watch this episode tonight, there's no way to avoid the spoilers.
C'mon, Lucy. Why don't you watch Valley of the Hidden with us? We can have movie night tomorrow.

You know I have my late class tomorrow.
PREVIOUSLY ON VALLEY OF THE HIDDEN: "OHMIGOD MY BABY! I CAN'T FIND IT, AND *GASP* IS THAT A UNICORN?!"

sigh

"I'M FROM THE FUTURE, AND I'M HERE TO..."

Wait, whose baby is missing?
No one's. Sally just thinks she had a baby, but it was really a hallucination.
Which one is Sally?
The blonde.

Oh. From your poster. I thought she got shot.
No, that was the other blonde.
And Virginia didn't get shot. It was a shape-shifter posing as her. She was in a coma in a well.

Who's that?
Carl.
Who's he?
All you need to know is he and Sally had a fling that no one knows about.

No way!
gasp
"AND YOU'RE BOTH THE FATHER!"

Wait, how can they BOTH be the father? This is ridiculous.
It's really great once you get into it.
Didn't you want to take a shower?

You got mail.

Dina Santiago
111 Montrose St
Meadville, NJ 07410
Amanda
17 Adams

That means the kid has a partial claim to the Unicorn King throne! Oh man! Melvin is going to FREAK OUT.

This. Is. Awe. Some.

Hey, Earth to half-unicorn man.

Sorry. I'm not feeling great. Mickey-D's isn't sitting right.

Ugh. Why do you eat that stuff?
Just trying to do my part to help the gas crisis.

Ewwww.

Wanna see the new Space Fleet movie on Saturday?

Why don't you see if Cat wants to go? You don't want an old fart—pun soon to be intended—hanging around.
BTW, cover your nose.

She hates any movie with science, no matter how many cute guys are in it.
Come on! I'll even wear my Vultronnian ears.

Sorry, Mads. I promised Father Tim I'd help with the soup kitchen.
How about Adam? Lord knows he'll follow you anywhere.

The soup kitchen?

I'll volunteer Saturday, too.
Sorry, no can do.

Why?
You'll be over your good deed limit. You're about to hit your quota by staying in this room.
Huh?

Oh God! My nose! It burns!
This week on Valley of the Hidden: when breaded chicken strips attack!

Keep that up and you'll kill the homeless this weekend. What time should I get there?
We really have too many hands. And, well, to be frank, if anything is going to kill them, it's your cooking.

Jerk.
Ha ha. Listen, you enjoy your weekend and that's final.
The show's back on!

So what. Dad had an affair with some tofu.

Jesus!

This face ain't big enough for the both of us, Zit.
Ugh. Can't they invent a cream that doesn't burn?

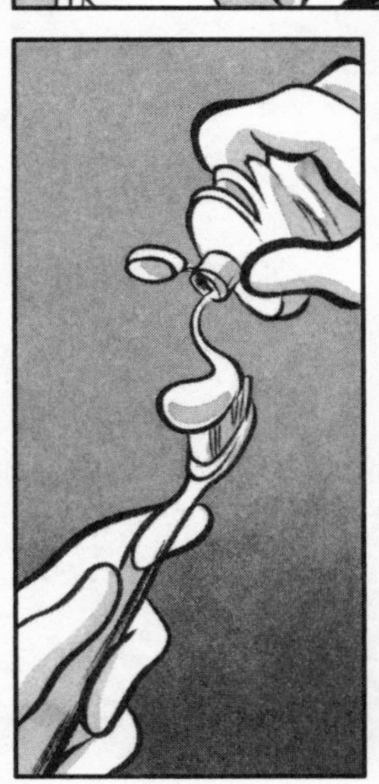

I can't believe Dina. She's got some nerve. Sending something to OUR house.
James, you're overreacting.

Amanda was going to find out sooner or later.
How the hell was she going to find out?
She's a smart girl.

I just don't want my daughter exposed to that.
YOUR daughter?

Don't make this about us.

CRASH

Go to bed!

Hi, it's Amanda. I know you forgive, so whatever Dad did, I should just forgive him, right? But he's lying. Can you make him tell me the truth? Or better yet, just make it so there's nothing to tell? Also, thanks for the zit. It's one of your more impressive ones. Amen.

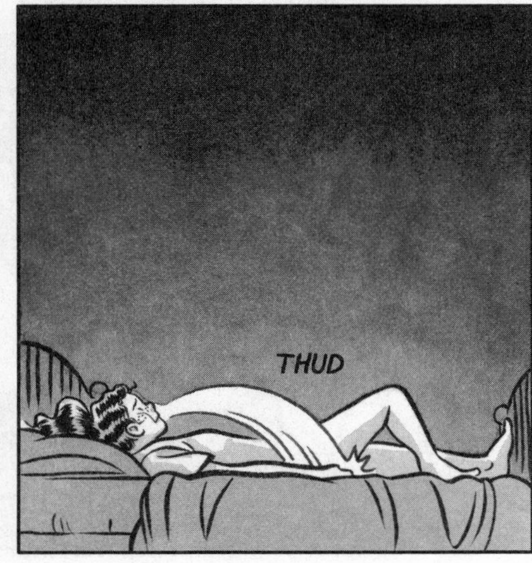
THUD

Good, you're up.
Why are you here? Isn't it Saturday?

Hello to you, too.
Sorry. But don't you have work?

Called in sick. Thought we could have a girls' day. Maybe check out a spa... mani-pedi, waxing...

Waxing is your idea of a fun day?
And I'm not forcing a stranger to smell my feet.

Okay. No spa.

How about we work on your driving?
No way. Took me three months to pay off the damage from last time. Besides, Cat has a license now.

Do you want to see if Cat's free to come with us?
She's grounded again.

Again? What did she do this time?
I plead the fifth, sixth, seventh, and any other amendment that gets me out of explaining.

Dad already go to the soup kitchen?

Did he...
Oh, yes.
Mom and Dad may be opposites, but they had one thing in common: they were both horrible liars.

I should talk with Cat's mom. Constantly grounded, but she doesn't learn.
The number of times I've seen her outside her house, necking in a parked car...
Necking? What're you, sixty?

I'm just saying I'm glad you calmed down with the boys.

Hey, what about Laura?
Laura's okay, but if we didn't live close I doubt we'd be friends at all.

AMANDA! That's horrible.
I mean, she's super nice... and boring... and clingy.
Just because she doesn't set things on fire and chase after boys doesn't make her a bad friend.

I didn't say she was a bad friend.
Then it's settled. I'll see if she's free.

CALL...
Um... I think I'm a little old for you to be arranging playdates.

Joann?
Haha. I know. I missed this month's meeting.
Jesus.
She didn't!? Well, that's not surprising.
Is Laura free for a visit?

Oh, great! Amanda and I are having a girls' day... My treat... Pick her up in a half hour?

Great! Laura's free. Come on, you've never had a mani-pedi. You might love it.
bzzzzzzz

Saved, like always, by my Cat in shining armor.
Poop. The Winstons need me to babysit today.
They can find someone else.

Everyone else is busy.
Besides, you keep telling me I should get a job.

I mean, that's true, but I was hoping... What about Laura...
I'll text Laura. I gotta get ready or I'll be late.

Bye!

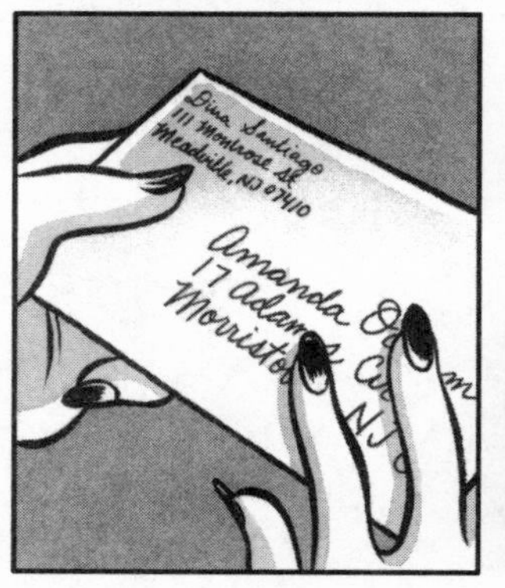
Dina Santiago
111 Montrose St
Meadville, NJ 07410
Amanda

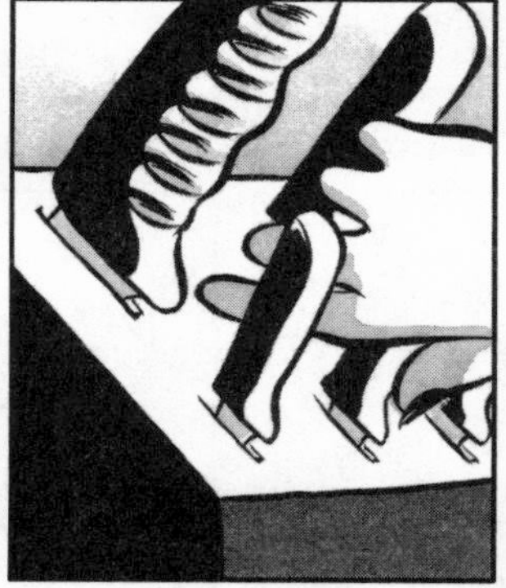

CINEMA
THE APARTMENT

CINEMA
THE APARTMENT

Your text saved my ass. Mom was driving me insane.
Super Bitch strikes again?

That's the weirdest part. She was being decidedly UN-bitchy.
Like, super nice instead, trying to make me hang out with Laura.
Said she thinks Laura's a good influence.

Laura's only a good influence if you need a sleep aid.
Hey! Did you hear, Vomit Train is playing a secret show at the Zipper tonight?

I thought you were grounded.
VOMIT TRAIN
the ZIPPE
Oh, I am, but Mom's working weekends.

So, did your dad meet up with Ms. Mystery Mistress today?
I don't want to talk about it.

Who's the vampire?
This super hot guy from Public. Jason.
Jimmy.
Jared?
Fred? Woodrow? Something like that.

Good to know he was memorable.
Maybe his NAME wasn't, but believe me, a part of him was DEFINITELY memorable.

Ewww.
It didn't go THAT far. But with him, hugging was more like stabbing.

La-la-la. So not listening.
If you were there maybe I wouldn't've missed curfew because of a guy whose name I can't remember. Come to the next party!

I'd get caught. Does it hurt?
Naw. Doesn't feel like anything.

Your mom won't find out. Besides, you're like a junior nun-in-training. When was your last date?

Seriously, it's been forever. I have trouble believing there's no one even worth CRUSHING on.

It's not my fault all the guys at our school suck.
So stop dating guys at our school. I did.

Though if Adam keeps this growth spurt going...
He's like our brother!

I always did like Flowers in the Attic.
Laura would FREAK.
That alone makes it worth it.

Doooooon't worry, I'll be good.
Besides, I think YOU should go for him.

He's too young.
It's two years!
I know him too well!
There are parts of him you've never met...
You're twisted.

I don't get you. He's hot. He's nice. He's totally in love with you. You're weird, Mads. You know that, right?

Crap, I've only got an hour to get ready. Meeting Paul for a movie.
Paul who? What movie?

So innocent.

Like it matters.

Sweet! Your mom's car is gone.
Thank God. That woman was gunning to wax me into a newborn.
Seen your legs recently? For once she mighta been doing you a favor.

Gotta go! Don't freak about your dad! I'm sure he didn't do anything.
Text me later! Love you!

I love you, too.

Patience has never been one of my strong points.

I used to think "a good imagination" was one of them...

...but I'm not so sure anymore.

click

Where were you?

You scared me! Why are you sitting in the dark?

Don't change the subject. Where were you?

What's the matter?
ANSWER THE QUESTION!

Why are you yelling?
Why are YOU wearing a suit to chop vegetables?

Well, the Gazette was doing a piece on the kitchen and they needed some of us to look nice and...
Stop lying! I know you cheated on Mom.

What?
I know about Dina. I'm a "smart girl."

Dina? Wait, you think...
Why did she want to see you today?

You don't know what you're talking about. Why aren't you out with your mom?
Mom was in on it?!

Mads, there are some things...
...it's better you don't know. Respect my privacy. It doesn't affect you.

Sit down. We're not done.

Sorry. I have to go and respect your privacy.

Amanda...
DON'T TOUCH ME!

Dammit.

BAM BAM BAM
Let me guess, forgot your key? Also, did you forget you were...

...grounded...

What are you doing here? Where the hell is Catherine?

Oh God, she's not hurt, is she?

Don't just walk away from me!

BAM BAM BAM BAM BAM BAM BAM

BAM BAM BAM
Coming. Coming.

Laura here?
She's upstairs. What's wrong?

Laura! Amanda's here.
Amanda?

What happened? Are you okay?
Do you need anything?
Are you cold?
You need socks.
Who hurt you?
I'll take care of it.
Stop attacking her.
I'm okay. I'm okay.
You can borrow a pair of mine.
I got in a fight with my dad.
Ohmigod, it's Saturday. Was it about...
Go away, Adam.
Sorry. I'll be in my room if you need anything.
Are you hungry at all? We just had...
ADAM!
I'm going. I'm going.

You still don't know it's true.
I know he was lying to me and my mom's in on it.

Can I borrow your phone?
Yeah, sure.

Pick up, pick up, pick up.
Who're you calling?

I'm busy, Laura. What do you want?

Oh, thank God!
Mads?
Where are you? Your mom is freaking out.

Lost track of time.
Figured if I was gonna get in trouble anyway I should make it worth it.

The punk showcase. Come! Come! Come!
THUD
Gerry's bouncing. I'll make sure he lets you in. Two-for-one ladies' specials!

Cat's at the Zipper. Can you give me a lift?
I don't know...
My parents will freak if I drive back by myself.

Then stay out with us.
No way. That place is super sketchy.
How are you even gonna get in?

Also... I mean...
I don't want to sound like a mom, but do you really think going there is a good idea?
You're upset. You need to talk it out, not get drunk at some sleazy club.
Take the stick out of your butt, Laura!

Please. I'll pay for gas.
I can drive you.
ADAM!

I wasn't listening. I just walked by.

Thank you. Thank you.

Maybe I should go.
No. It's okay. I know you don't want to. Also, I'm not sure Cat could sneak more than one of us in.

Let's go.
sigh
You aren't going there with bare feet.

Tie 'em tight. It'll be one more layer for the rapists to get through.

You saved me tonight.
Whatever. Just don't get killed.

So, what happened?
Long story.

I've got time.
Short version: My dad's a liar. My mom's an idiot. The end.

Listen, I really don't feel like going into it.
But thanks.
It's cool. I understand.

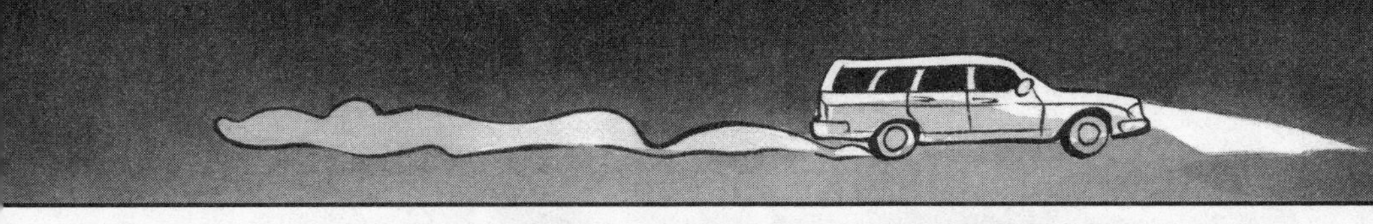

Oh, hey! Did you hear? I made varsity, only sophomore on the team.
That's really great.

Well, they were shorthanded, so they kinda had to bump me up, but it's still an honor.

I've been running a lot. Started lifting some weights. I don't know if you can tell.
No, you can totally tell.

Mads...
...by any chance do you...
Mind if I turn on the radio?

What?
Oh. No. Yeah. I like music.

PIZZA

sigh

ZIPPERS
For a night you may never remember!
Live music every night!
Saturday is Ladies Night!

Wait. Stop.
ZIPP

What?
I should get out here. If they see me getting dropped off, they'll know I'm not twenty-one.

Maybe they'll figure you're a twenty-one-year-old who never got a license 'cause she kept driving into sationary objects?

Haha. Very funny.
You can't help it. It's not like parked cars stay still.

Sorry. Just wanted to see you smile.
Be careful. Here, take my phone.
No. No, I can't.

Fine. Don't take it.

I'll leave it here in case you change your mind.

VRRROOOOM
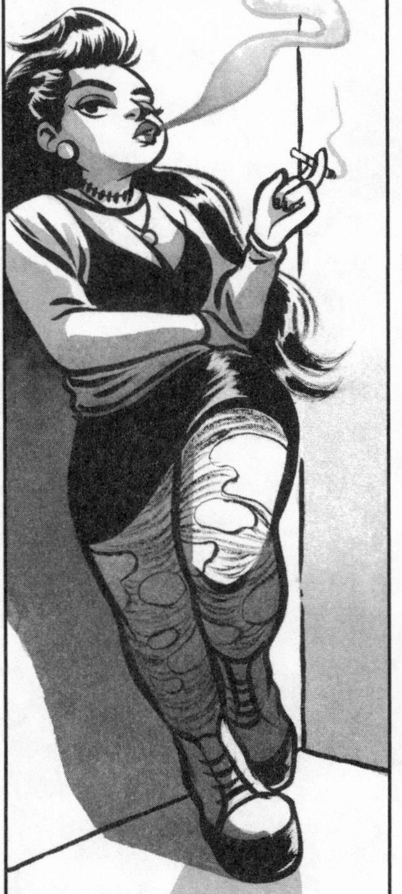

There you are! Gerry, Mads. Mads, Gerry.
Hi.
grunt

So this is the infamous Zipper?
Normally it's as shitty as it looks, but not tonight! Vomit Train's here!

They're actually playing?
You're gonna love 'em. Electro-punk with a girl lead on keys. Like the bastard child of MSI and Dresden.

Two PBRs!
How old is she?

I said two PBR's.

Fine. It's not my ass.

Oh, lighten up, Chris.
Here. Don't push your luck. You're a lightweight if I ever saw one.

Ever since Chris decided he wanted to be a cop, he's been a total douche.
That guy's a cop?!
Naw. He keeps failing the test.
Hey, I wanna introduce you to some people.
There you are, baby. Been looking for you. Who's your *burp*
Yeah. Not him.

Jess, Rick, Ken'ichi...
This is my best friend, Amanda.
Just call me K.
Hi.
We've heard all about you. I'm so glad you finally came!

What happened to Paul?
Blah. Paul.
Where are they? Didn't take their egos long to blow up. Fuckin' hype.
K's just pissed since their band got bumped.

We didn't get bumped. They overscheduled.
The booker screwed up.
Yeah, seven bands is totally fine, but eight, now THAT would have been too many.

Fuck this. I'm buying shots...
Woo!
Sweet!
...for everyone but you two.

What'll it be, new girl?
Um. I'm not really into shots.
All right, all right! We're sorry!
Sorry their band is so bad?

HAHAHAHAHAHAHA HAHA

Where're Nate and Darren?
Prolly off somewhere being gay.

Whaaaat. It's true!
Who're they?
Darren is Jess's brother. Nate's a guitar player for a coupla bands.

You guys all go to Public?
Public?
She means Morristown.

Yeah, graduated last year. I always forget you go to that weird little private school.
Catholic school. With uniforms. I don't forget.

Awww, I knew you couldn't stay mad at us!
Fat chance, jerks.
Extras are for me and the new girl.

She looks like she's had the same kinda day I've had.

Kanpai, assholes.
KANPAI!

Jesus was all into turning water into wine.

They probably just forgot to write about all the times he changed water into tequila.

Well, SHE'S my best friend when she's not sucking face with some idiot, but he was ALWAYS my best friend.

Look at Jess. Dancing like it has a beat or something. Traitor.

HA HAHAHA
HA H
Heh
heh

KISS NUMBER 6

Close your eyes, Amanda.
Close your eyes.

How the hell can someone so little weigh so much? What did she drink?
Um...just...

A lot. Hahaha!
I think I liked you better when you were a preachy straight edge.

You're so pretty. Isn't Cat pretty?

Snap out of it. I can handle MY mom, but there's no way I can handle yours.

Those aren't my shooooes.

Where am I?
Um...about thirty seconds away from being grounded for life.

Breaking the law, breaking your curfew, coming home at three in the morning drunk out of your mind, vomiting on the lawn!

Want me to keep going?

What about you?
Oh, I'm pretty sure I didn't do any of those things at your age.

No, I mean, what about YOU. Lying to me, trying to make sure I didn't find out about Dina.
"Girls' Day," my ass!

You just gonna let Dad get away with it?
I don't know where you got this insane idea. Dina is not who you think she is.

Then who the fuck is she?
Amanda!

You're seriously not going to tell me?!
It's not my choice to make.

Oh, grow a backbone.
FRANCO

Okay, God. I get it. And you're making sure my stomach and I both don't forget it.

But shouldn't there be some rating system for sins?

Like drunken lawn puking. That's maybe a 2.5 on a scale of 10.

Maybe only a 2 if it's raining out.

Our father...
Murder: 10 points. Stealing: 4 points.
Putting an ice cream container back in the freezer empty: 6 points because that's just cruel.
Lord's name in vain: 0 points. C'mon, you were kidding about that one, right?

...who art in heaven...
Lying, cheating, adultery, more lying...

...hallowed be thy name...
Maybe this scale needs to go to 11.

Hey, Mads. See you at the game?
She's grounded.

You don't happen to know how Amanda wound up drunk last night wearing your sister's shoes?
I, uh...

Leave him alone. Laura and Adam tried to stop me, so I hitched.
YOU HITCHED!? Jesus, this just keeps getting better.

Hmmmf!
Oh, please.
James!

They pull another one like last time, I'm skipping the Nighthawks game. No way I'm driving way out there to watch them sleep on the field.
You're all talk, Sal. You'd never skip a game.

I'm not made of gas money!
Just made of gas.
They lose today...I boycott away games.
I'll drive you.

Haha. You've had your license for what, twenty seconds?
Three weeks, and actually he's a great driver. Winds up the Xbox was good for something.

I'm also really good at the flight simulator games.

Don't push it.

Where's lady luck?
Grounded and hopefully still feeling like death. She came home drunk.
Drunk!?

That's not like Amanda.
Let me guess, she was with Catherine? That girl needs some serious parental attention.

I got to watch my sweet, innocent daughter fall out of a cab and shoot her dinner all over our front yard.
At least they were smart enough to take a cab.

Eh, think of all the stuff you did at her age.
That's not the point. SHE was raised right.

Jim, your mom was Mary Poppins on steroids. I swear she spent every day making us cookies, always hot out of the oven.
Almost as hot as she was.
Ha!
I had the biggest crush.
Gross, Dad.

What the hell is your point?
I'm saying you were raised just fine, but I could write a book with all the dumb drunken things we did.
You're being too hard on her. It's just part of growing up.

Wow. I'm lucky I know such an expert...
...oh, wait, I forgot, you don't have any kids.

Holy crap.
They're starting Franco?! He hasn't started in six years!
I'm gonna go.

That came out harsher than I meant.
No. I know how you meant it. I'm gonna go.

Amanda's a good kid. You wanna be your father, I'm not going to stop you, but if you ever, EVER resort to his style of discipline, I swear to God—
I'd never do that. You know that!

Mads woulda been really happy to see this.
FRANCO
40

Hey! Why didn't you call me back yesterday?
Phone, computer, TV, freedom—all gone.
AND I have to work the soup kitchen the next four Saturdays.

God, I love my mom. By the time I got home, she was so drunk she didn't even notice.
This sucks.

Well, at least you had fun with K.
K?

Um, yeah...
...you know, the guy you were making out with for like FOREVER?
I kissed K?!

No, you didn't kiss him. You devoured his face.
For like THREE hours.

Shit, I don't remember that at all.
PHYSICS

I remembered pieces. Cat and Rick. I remembered Cat and Rick.

Amanda?
Yeah.
Your father tells me you'll be helping out at the kitchen. We're thrilled to have you.

Sister Clara, was my dad there Saturday?

BRRRRRRIIING

Your father was doing important work last weekend.

All right, Act II, Scene 1. I need a Polonius, a Reynaldo, and an Ophelia.
Lying nuns? Maybe there's no such thing as a good person.

Forget something?

Crap, the mail. Sorry. Though haven't you been home for hours...
AMANDA.

Take out the trash while you're at it.
Fiiine.

?

for Amanda
Holy shiiiii...
...thirty thousand dollars...
CINEMA
THE APARTMENT
Bank
CASHIER'S CHECK
AMANDA ORHAM
$30,000.00

Your grandfather loved you very much.
Don't tell your parents about this. They would not approve.
Don't tell your parents?

Anything for me?
Crap, the mail.

Sorry. Sorry.
Honestly, Amanda! God gave you a brain, and I'd suggest you start using it.

I've got homework.
No computer. Don't forget you're grounded.
Couldn't forget if I tried. And you took the power cord.

CINEMA

CINEMA
THE APARTMENT

CINEMA
THE APARTMENT

Whoever he is, he's hot.
Don't joke. I'm completely freaked out.
CINEMA

Thirty thousand and your parents have no idea! You're always so damn lucky!
I'm not touching that money.

WHAT!
I don't know where it came from! Who this guy is... what he has to do with one of my grandpas...
...and the whole "don't tell your parents" thing. You can't tell me that's not a molester catchphrase.

Molester catchphrase?
Don't worry about it.
Check this out!

Don't—

What's this?
It's enough money to start our own record label...
...ohhh, or buy one of those diamond-covered bras. Bling boobs!

I found it in the trash yesterday.
The trash? Is this your grandpa?

No idea who that is. And could the note on the back be more cryptic?
Crazy, right?
CINEMA
THE APARTMENT

CINEMA
THE APARTMENT

Well, that's partially because someone added the bottom line.

Wait, what?

Go to the bank, ask them if it's real. If it's real, then WOO-HOO!

If it's fake, oh well, must be some Nigerian prince taking a handwriting class.

I don't have their numbers, but I could sneak home...
Skipping? You're already grounded.
It's Mr. Stewart. I'll just say your name and the magic word: "tampon."

Use the door by the gym.
The "alarm" beeps really quietly and only for maybe ten seconds.
Time it with the bell and you're golden.
It locks, so make sure to prop it to get back in.
EMERGE

What would I do without you?
Die a horrible slow death of boredom.

Can you hold on to this? I'm worried about my parents finding out I have it.

Sure.

RGENCY EXIT

BRRRRRRRIIING
Beep. Beep. Beep.

Okay, God: skipping class. What do you think, a 4 on the scale?
Maybe only 3?

Hello?

Dad work
Mom work
Grandma + Grandpa SUTTER
Grandma + Grandpa ORHAM
Mads school

Hello?
Mandy! How are you?
Hey, Grandpa. It's Mandy.
Doris, it's Mandy.
How sweet!

Is Grandma okay?
Sort of. I think she put her head in the pet store hamster cage. Bunch of wheels stuck in there.

Graham! Haha. He always makes that joke when I have it in rollers.
Hasn't gotten old yet! Unlike us!

How are you? Still getting those good grades?
I'm doing okay. Precalc is a little rough.
Don't tell her I snitched, but your mother was a straight-C student no matter what we tried! Always more into fashion than being fashionably on time to class.

You have the day off of school?
Oh...uh... I get special honor society privileges.

No kidding! We didn't even have an honor society. I remember St. Francis being a prison. Spent four years trying to remember what crime I committed.
Probably doing time for bad jokes.
Haha.

So, what's the occasion?
I just. Um. I wanted to thank you for the gift.
Oh, that? It was nothing.

Are you kidding? It's the best thing anyone ever gave me! But what's with the picture?
Oh no! Did I buy the wrong format DDV?
DVD, honey. DVD.

DVD?
Truth be told, I had no idea what to get you, but your dad told me you were really into that show Hills and Valleys.
It's Valley of the Hidden.
I thought I would buy you some tapes of it.
Discs, honey, not tapes.
Mandy knows what I mean!

So sweet of you to call, especially since you already sent a card. Do you know you're the only grandkid who ever sends thank-you cards?

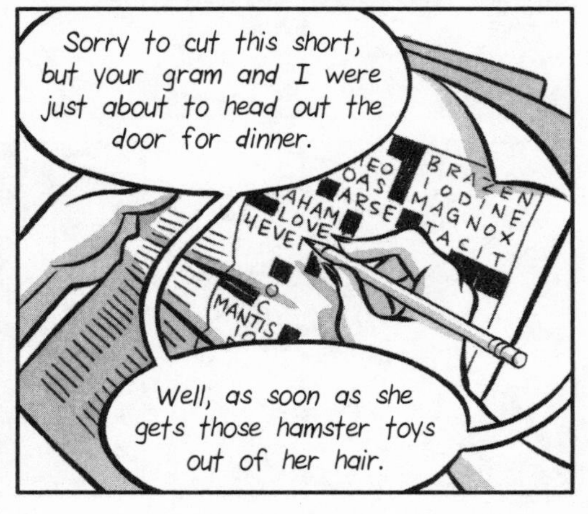
Sorry to cut this short, but your gram and I were just about to head out the door for dinner.
Well, as soon as she gets those hamster toys out of her hair.

Next time your mom calls, steal the phone. I want to hear more about your junior year. I'm sick of hearing about her Piraties classes.
Pilates, dear.
Oh, I know. Jim called it that once. Made me laugh so hard I almost had to swab the deck. Haha.

Swab the... Oh, that's disgusting, Graham.
I imagine she teaches it with an eye patch and peg leg.
Haha.

You're insane.
And you love me.
Haha. Maybe.

All right, we're off. Love you!
I love you, too.

That narrowed it down...but didn't make the next call any easier.

1
Mom work
2
Grandma + Grandpa SUTTER
3
Grandma + Grandpa ORHAM
Mads school
5

Ring... Ring... Ring...

There was a line of command. If I wanted to talk to Grandpa or Grandma O, I went through Dad.
Ring... Ring... Ring... Ring... Ring... Ring...
INCOMING CALL
TALK

Me calling them direct was like throwing a grappling hook over the pearly gates to avoid St. Peter.
Only instead of some nice omnipresent dude on a fancy chair on the other side, there's just a bitter old man and his trophy wife.

Click.

You've reached the residence of Dr. Robert Orham, PhD, and Mrs. Robert Orham. Leave a message after the tone with your name, number, and reason for your call. We will return your call if we deem it appropriate.
No sales calls.

BEEP.
...

They're still on the cruise...

Shit.

Oof.
Adding "a track team" to my list of things I wish St. Francis had.
SAINT FRANCIS CATHOLIC HIGH SCHOOL

EXIT ONLY

Hello, Amanda.
Aahh!

Jesus, you scared me!
You must be new to skipping.
The military crawl thing only works in sitcoms.

A goody-goody like you is an expert on skipping?
The goody-goody role I leave for Laura.
I'm waging a war against the cafeteria. Went to Whole Foods and got a cheese plate today.
I guess you could say I'm more of a gouda-gouda.

Heh. I gotta run.
Thanks for covering for me Saturday.
Least I could do.
Oh, and if you aren't busy...
...I mean, I know you aren't busy since you're grounded...
...but if you aren't THAT grounded you should come to our game tomorrow.

Maybe your dad would be cool with it if you, like, volunteer as scorekeeper or dress up as our mascot...
St. Francis has a mascot?

Well, no, but maybe that's our problem.
I don't think I can. Sorry!

Gouda-gouda?! Smooth, Adam.

So it wasn't either grandpa?
Definitely wasn't either, and I think I pulled an ass muscle running. This day sucks.

Where are we going?
You'll see.

West Point Savings Bank
Check it out.

I'm just going to wait here.

Why?
I just...I just feel more comfortable out here.
Whatever.

W P S B
West Point Saving
JESS

Cat! New girl!
How the hell are you?
Better once we cash this bad boy.

Wow.
Did someone die?
JES

She doesn't want to talk about it.
OH, SHIT! When am I going to learn to stop making that joke?!

Don't worry. No one died.
I didn't know you worked here.
I work here FOR NOW—until the band takes off. Or I "prove myself" and get to go back to college. My parents totally freaked after I failed, like, two classes.

K will be super jealous. He keeps trying to find a way to accidentally run into you.
Do you have your account info?
Uh...yeah. Here.

Haha!
A Mula-Mula account? What are you, ten?
Mula-Mula! Kids-Like Save Money!
Smart choice for Savers 5-18

You going to the all-ages show? I know K would love that, and I love anything that shuts him up.
I'm like twelve varieties of grounded after last time.
Also, K is nice and all, I mean, from what I remember, but...

No need. K is K.
Here, fill this out.
He's not boyfriend material unless you're a fan of fine whines. W-H-I-N-E-S. Ha!
JESS
Sign here. I'll be right back.

W P S B
Point
Change can start with CHANGE!
Can't believe Jess works here. I'd kill myself.
It doesn't seem bad. Better than McDonald's.

No, this is worse. This is the kind of thing you think is temporary, then thirty years go by and you're still wearing a pin with a cartoon monster eating pennies.
It's like throwing your life away at nineteen...

Ugh. Look at Laura. She drives me crazy.
Scared to come into a bank?
Walking around like she's better than us.

You know, I think I might hate her!

She's not that bad.
Yes. Yes, she is. You agree with me, right, Botox Lady?

Soooo, what are we gonna do if it's real?
Her nose? I'm pretty sure it's not real.

You're lucky I like you.
If the check's real, I'll probably do the same thing as if it's fake, i.e., be really weirded out by the whole thing and go home.

Bad news, guys.
For trying to cash this illegal check you actually OWE forty-five dollars.
WHAT?!

Haha! Sorry, couldn't resist. Naw, it's all cool. 100 percent legit. It'll take a few days for the funds to be available.

You're always such a lucky bitch.

Okay. Account's all set! Now go buy some f'ing records! Preferably mine.
The record's done?
Of course not, but maybe this decade!

Jessica...
I'm just about done, Mrs. Cline.

See you at the showcase?
We'll be there!

NEXT.

Change can start with CHANGE!
W P S B

Savings Bank
WP
Sorry, I got a little nervous. How did it—
Grow some balls, Laura.
Now go away. We have grown-up things to talk about.

It happened every few months.
SAINT FRANCIS

Cat would lose it with Laura and snap over something stupid.

And Laura always took it. Never said a word. Just pretended it never even...
Why do you have to be so horrible all the time?

At least I have a personality, Whitebread.
Cat, let it go.
No. I won't.
Laura, you're boring. You never have anything to say unless you're playing mom or nun. Do you think we CHOOSE to hang out with you?
Cat!
What's that supposed to mean?

Our parents practically beg us to hang around you in the hopes your perfectness will rub off on us like social leprosy.
If you didn't live in the development, there's no way we'd be friends.
That's not true.
You're such a liar. You say it all the time.
"Laura puts me to sleep."
"Laura's so boring."
"Laura wouldn't know a good time if it bit her on the ass."

Don't listen to her.
Oh, you are so full of shit.

Laura, come back!

Why the hell did you have to do that?
I'm sick of her hanging around. Why do we put up with her?
I mean, she obviously can't stand me, so the only thing I can come up with is that she must be in love with you or something. I just...
I just feel like she exists to make ME feel like a worse person.

Not that this is helping. See! She still wins! Ugh!
This is so going to get back to my parents. Thanks a lot.

Nice. Way to make this all about you. I almost forgot it's ALWAYS about you.

Why did you tell Jess I was going to the show?
Because you are going to sneak out of the house after your parents go to sleep. OBVIOUSLY.

That's not even funny.
Good. Because it wasn't a joke.
You're buying drinks this time. Even if you don't want to use any of the mystery money, I bet you can blackmail your dad and his mistress—

What nooow?

Why don't you ever know when to stop?

First you're a total bitch to Laura—
—who may be boring, but she didn't deserve that—
—and to top it all off you don't seem to give a shit about how upset I've been this week!

You're supposed to be my best friend, but you don't care that I'm scared my parents are going to get divorced...
...and that my dad's cheating...
...and that I just cashed a check from a mysterious stranger who maybe now thinks I owe them something!
I care!
I care that "Oh no, your perfect dad's maybe not so perfect"...
...and "Oh no, people are sending you large amounts of money."
I totally care!
Mads, you're my best friend and it's my right to tell you when you're overreacting.
You. Are. Overreacting.
Your life is cake.

So, I know I said no TV, but I was talking to Sal and I realized maybe I'm being too hard on you.
Besides, a new Valley of the Hidden is on.
Wouldn't be the same without my...

ARRRRRG!

Arg? Did you go to Mom's Piraties class?
That joke wasn't funny the first ten times.

Listen, Mads. I love you and I know you've had a rough week, but you have to understand—
Who's Dina?
Are you still convinced I have some mistress? I would never cheat.
Tell me or get out of my room.

Dina...
...Dina's just...
...a close friend of my mother's.
Nope. Not good enough. Get out.

Don't bother DVRing Valley of the Hidden. I'm not watching it anymore.
The last two seasons have sucked anyway.

Okay. Snapping at my dad: that's probably only like 2 points. Talking behind Laura's back: 5, maybe 6? Wishing Cat would call me and we'd make up even though I know she is totally in the wrong: I mean, it's forgiveness, so maybe I win points?

I know. Even I'm not buying it.

click
Finally.

I'm only five minutes late.
Where's Amanda?
I thought we decided she could watch the show?
She still won't talk to me.

Serves you right.
Whose side are you on?
The side that tells your daughter the truth.

I can't. I just...I mean, it took me ten years before I even told you!
Well, you've known her for seventeen years, so it's overdue.

I know you went through a lot, and it breaks my heart, but your mother's actions have nothing to do with her.

Are you worried because of how she is with Cat?
What?
Um...never mind.

This whole thing is such a mess. I should just tell her. Right?
You need to tell her.
That's what I've been saying.

Okay, I'll tell her about the affair...
...eventually...
...but for now let's shred the letter. I don't want Amanda to have anything to do with them or that money.

God. That picture. It gives me chills. We should burn it.

About the letter...
I feel like my head is going to explode.

Sorry. I cut you off—what were you saying?

You should go lie down. You've had a rough couple of days.

Jim...

Yeah.

I'm sorry about what happened. I am.
Your parents had problems, but don't you think she deserves the gift?
It could mean the difference between her going to local college or a school that might actually give her a future.

No. We shred it. We'll get the money some other way.
Promise me you'll talk to her. Explain about Dina... and Sam...

No. I'm sorry, but no.

God, if it's possible, and I'm not sure it is, please be kind to Sam...

...wherever she might have wound up.

GIMMEGIMMES

knock knock
What do you want?

Ugh. I'm trying to read!

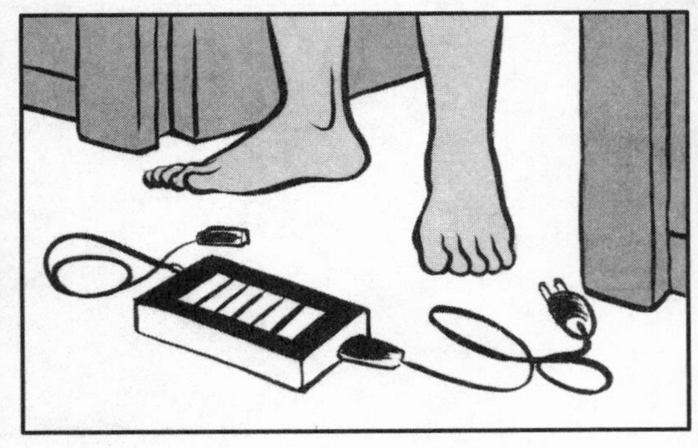

chiiime

Oh, good.

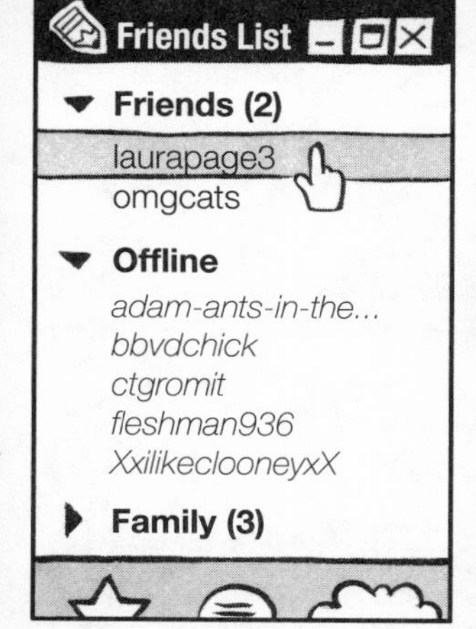
Friends List
Friends (2)
laurapage3
omgcats
Offline
adam-ants-in-the...
bbvdchick
ctgromit
fleshman936
XxilikeclooneyxX
Family (3)

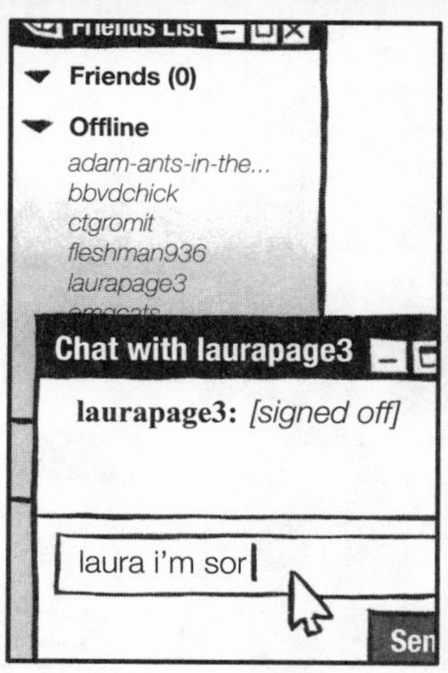
Friends (0)
Offline
adam-ants-in-the...
bbvdchick
ctgromit
fleshman936
laurapage3
Chat with laurapage3
laurapage3: [signed off]
laura i'm sor

Bing.

Chat with laurapage3
laurapage3: [signed off]
laurapage3: [signed on]

MadVOTH: laura! i thought you just blocked me i'm so so sorry about today. cat didn't mean what she said
laurapage3: sorry mads. it's adam. laura must have her password saved. i should sign off.
MadVOTH: no wait don't! i need to talk to you. you have a minute?

laurapage3: sure. of course. let me just switch accounts. laura would kill me if she caught me on here.
MadVOTH: k

Accept message from Hojo86?
Ignore
Accept

MadVOTH: what happened to "adam-ants-in-the-pants"
Hojo86: my crazy aunt just discovered the internet and chats me constantly. you catch the new reference?
MadVOTH: um... is it some obscure band only cat would know about?

Hojo86: wow for someone who practically lives baseball you don't know your history
Hojo 1986, Howard Johnson 3-baseman for the Mets when they kicked ass in 1986???

Hojo86: hey I actually have some tickets to a Mets game in a few weeks and chris totally bailed on me. want to come?
MadVOTH: i'm not much of a major league fan but thanks hey is your sister there?

Hojo86: um...kinda.

Hojo86: she just stormed upstairs i'm not complaining since it means i get the computer i really need to get my own computer

MadVOTH: so right after i signed on?

Hojo86: it was probably just a coincidence
she might have read an article about a hurt puppy
or maybe found a piece of bad grammar on nytimes.com.
you know how sensitive she is about commas.

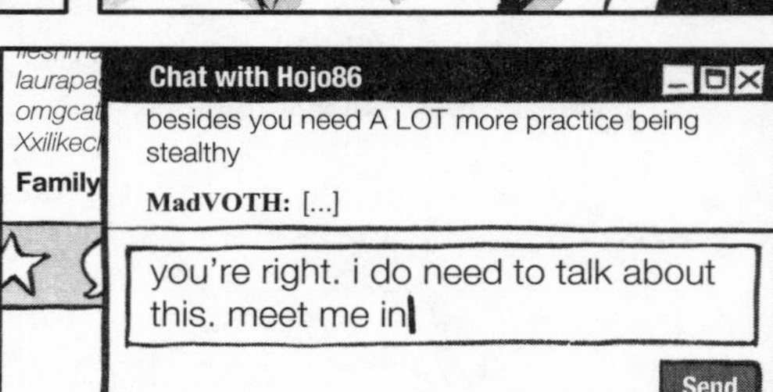

MadVOTH: i'm fine. when you see laura tell her I'm sorry. gotta go.
Hojo86: wait! if you're on the computer again does this mean you aren't grounded anymore?
MadVOTH: seems that way
Hojo86: great! then you can come to the game. we're really better this year. have a good chance of winning. cat already signed the both of you up as gamekeepers anyways.
MadVOTH: doubt she'll show. cat hates me right now, too.
Hojo86: naw she'll be there. She never misses a game.
MadVOTH: really? weird. i can never get her to watch baseball
Hojo86: coulda fooled me. you get some rest. see you tomorrow! sweet dreams. don't let whatever it is that's bugging you bite!
MadVOTH: thanks
sigh
knock knock

Amanda = officially ungrounded. I love you -DAD
P.S. For being so lazy, that Cat is annoyingly persistent.
37 Messages
Thirty-seven voicemails?
beep beep
beep
Monday, 5:33 P.M. Pick up. Pick up. Pick up. Geez, are you STILL grounded?
Monday, 6:02 P.M. I'm bored. Think I'll learn to break-dance. If I hurt myself tell your dad it's all his fault that you weren't here to stop me.
Monday, 6:03 P.M. Ow. Did you know it's a lot harder to spin on your head than it looks on TV?
Monday, 6:18 P.M. Ohmigod, Mandy. Did you see what Mimi was wearing to school today? Oh yeah... IT WAS THE SAME THING WE ALL ALWAYS WEAR! I'm sick of uniforms. It makes it so much harder to be a catty bitch.
Monday, 7:02 P.M. I'm beginning to think these messages are being checked by your dad. Mr. Orham, can you hear this? If so you're getting sleepy...veeeeery sleepy. When I snap my fingers you will unground your daughter and buy her an ice-cream cake to ask for forgiveness. One of those ones with the cookie crumbles in the middle. And she can share it only with her very hot best friend Cat. *snap*

BRRRRRRRRRRRRIIIIIIIIIIINNNG
sigh

This is going to be a long day.

BRRRRRRRRRRRRIIIIIIIIIIIIINNNG
And don't forget the quiz on Monday.

Laura...

I'm gonna be late.
I'm sorry. Cat was being an idiot.
So was I.
I told her off afterward and, well... now both of you aren't talking to me.

She's right, though. We don't make sense as friends. I don't even know why I didn't go in the bank. I just...
I just got nervous. I always feel like the third wheel.

Laura, you're one of my best friends.

So, I did some research on the photograph. It's the Guibert Theater in Meadville. The movie playing was The Apartment, you know, the one where Jack Lemmon makes spaghetti with a tennis racket. I IMDBed and it came out in 1960.

Thank you, thank you, thank you.

I found out more about the picture, too... I think I know who it is.
Who?
No, wait, don't tell me now. I want the full story. Library after school?

Sounds good... and thanks. After yesterday...
I don't want to talk about yesterday anymore.

12
3
BRRRRRRIII

Whoa, you got here fast.
Told Ms. White that I needed some library time to work on my research paper on the Spanish-American War.

How's the paper going?
Oh, I finished that a week ago.

So, what did you find out about him?

I'm pretty sure my grandmother had an affair with him. I'm also pretty sure his name is Sam, and that woman Dina is somehow connected to this. They mentioned her a few times. I couldn't figure out why.
Whoa. This keeps getting weirder.

Let me just go get some old Gazettes from 1960. I figure that's a good place to start. And maybe track down some census information. Meadville is still pretty small. Bet there can't be that many Samuels living there in 1960.
See, this is why it's good to have genius friends!

I kept feeling phantom buzzes.

I was so used to Cat sending me messages all day long.

sigh

This is a lot less like a CSI montage than I hoped.
Nothing. Not even microfilm. Our library sucks.

Everything sucks here. Our library, the teachers, the other students, our sports teams...

Crap! That reminds me. I told Adam I'd go to his game.
Don't go.

You'll only lead him on. The other night I caught him asking you out in the mirror.
No way.

It's true! He was using a British accent. It was... painful.

Besides, we have a mystery to solve.

I'd feel guilty ditching Adam. I mean, he's been super helpful lately.
Helpful?
Driving you to a bad club so you can make out with some stranger and then throw up on your lawn?
Yeah. So helpful.

I also really need to talk to Cat. She's scorekeeping.

I thought you were mad at her.
She didn't mean it. She's my best friend...

...one of my best friends. I can't handle her being mad at me.

C'mon, Adam will be happy to have his big sis there.
No. As much as he drives me crazy, I hate watching them lose. Besides, he'll blame it on me. I think Sal's superstitions are rubbing off on him.

Thanks again for trying to help. I'll see you later.

AWAY
INNING
HOME
02
1
00
CRACK!

2 to 0? Could be worse...
It's the top of the first!
Wow, really? This is much better than their usual!

"Top of the first"? Since when do you know anything about baseball?
Since number 7.

Knights

Wow, really running out of guys, aren't you?
Wrong number 7.

St. Francis

At least wait until he finishes puberty before you corrupt him and make web-footed babies.
Oh, he's done with puberty and he's done well.

Geez. Keeping score is depressing.
What did you expect? These other schools have thousands of students.
We have thirty-five guys per grade and a quarter of the guys are nerds who're here because they kept getting beat up at Public.
We need a bigger pool.

You'd look pretty good as a guy. You volunteering?

HAHAHAHAHA

Isn't this partially a game of luck? You'd think at some point the big G would toss a mini-miracle our way considering we're a Catholic school.
Yeah... maybe.

Just not today.

Good game.
Good game.
Good play.
Nice game.
Good game.
Nice game.
St. Francis

Well, six innings isn't too bad. Yay, fifteen-run rule.
Aren't they supposed to slap butts? Why don't they slap butts?

SLAP BUTTS!

Hey.

Fifteen-run rule.
Figured.
ST FRANCIS HIGH SCHOOL

Laura...I was totally PMSing and took it out on you. Sorry.

I found out where we could get the list of residents of Meadville.
Uh... Apology accepted? Circle yes or no? No writing "maybe."

Apology accepted. Like I was saying, we just need to go to the town clerk and look up the records. So, are you free on Saturday?

Sure.
Yay! Wait...What are we talking about?

Laura figured out that picture was taken in Meadville in 1960.
Whoa. I was kidding about it before, but really, you are a total Velma!

You free Saturday?
Can't. I've gotta hang out with my dad. The dick skipped the last few months.
...

What about Sunday?
It's only open on Saturdays.
Oh.

It's cool. I'll just have to wait to hear the exciting story of espionage and local government filing systems.

8 SOUTH
Meadville

Ring Ring
Mr. Orham, it's bad enough you take Amanda's phone, but now you're making prank calls on it. I can assure you my refrigerator hates exercise.

I forgot to tell you last night. Guess who's ungrounded?
gasp Elvis?! I always knew he was still alive!

How's things with your dad?
As expected. He keeps making lame excuses. You in Meadville yet?
Almost. Just wanted to call and say hi.

Hi.
Hi.

Now go and solve some mysteries, Scooby! Later! *click*

There it is.

MEADVILLE CITY CLERK

ding-a-ling-aling

Um...hi...we need to, uh...talk to the city clerk?
That's me! What can I do ya for?

We need resident data. Like, from the past. 1960?
Gertie, get the book!

This for a school report? A report about Meadville? Meadville's a great town. Used to be full of silver mines. Well, just one, but it was a great one.
GERTIE! You get that data yet?

Can't take it with you, but you can use the photocopier over there—twenty-five cents a copy, worth it for the history.
WHUMP!

Do you have addresses and names of residents?
Meadvil
Gazette

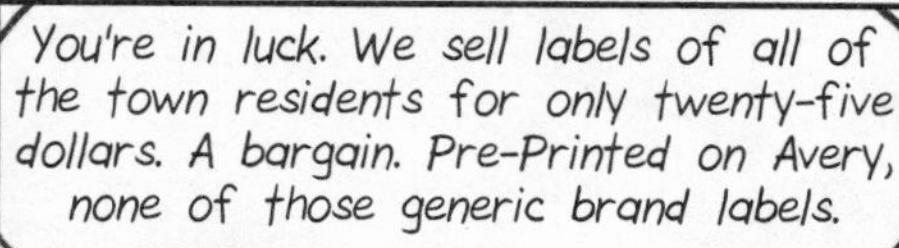
You're in luck. We sell labels of all of the town residents for only twenty-five dollars. A bargain. Pre-Printed on Avery, none of those generic brand labels.

Great for a Girl Scout cookie campaign or Little League popcorn fund-raisers.
What do you say? You want a set?

Do you have a list from 1960?
Why would you want a mailing list from 1960? Avery didn't exist in 1960. Or did they?
Gertie! Look that up: When was the Avery label company founded?

You going to buy the labels or not? I'm a busy man.
Is there an easier way to search this, like maybe digitally?

I don't have time for this. Gertie, get these kids out of here.

Well, that was a total waste of gas. What a jerk!

Ahem.

Meadville Population
Census: 1960

Yes! This is perfect!
How much do we owe you?

CITY CLERK
Avery labels, my ass.

Do you see many Sams on there?
I'm having trouble reading in the car. The type is so small!

DINER
There's a diner. Want to just go there?
Good idea.

Hi. Two.
Welcome, girls. Want a booth or a...

MENU

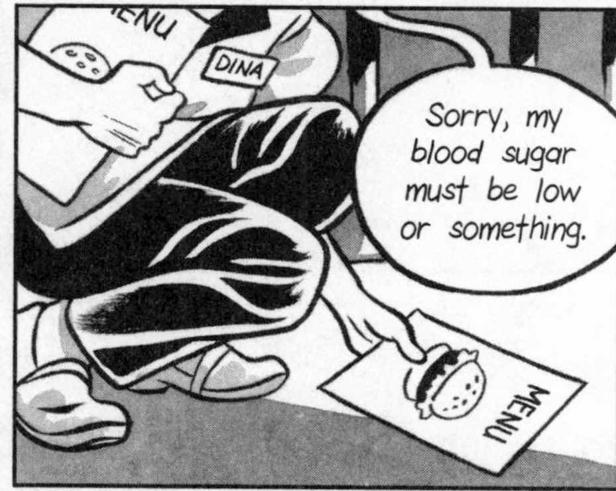
DINA
Sorry, my blood sugar must be low or something.
MENU

MENU

What'll it be?
Mozzarella sticks.
Coke. Diet.

Great. Big spenders.

Okay, you take that half and I'll take this one. Circle any Sams you find.

Nabor, Margaret
Nadelbach, Samuel

Garfield,
Garfield
Getty,

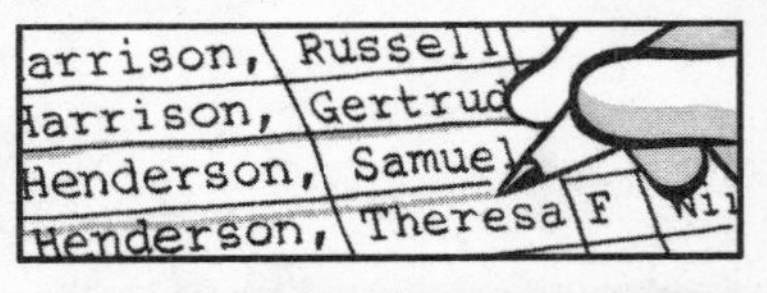
Russell
Harrison,
Henderson, Samuel
Henderson, Theresa F

Okay. That's weird.

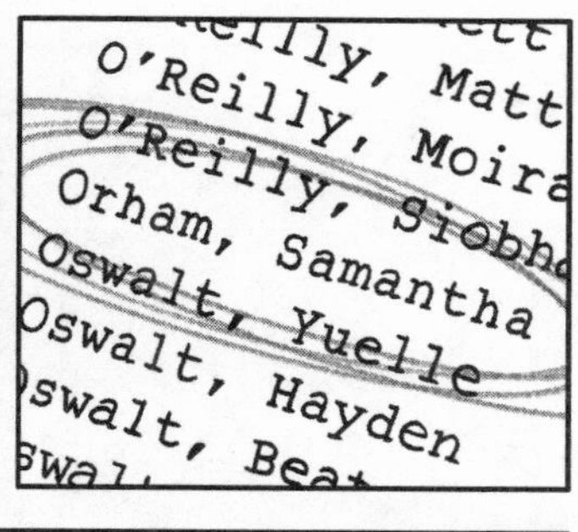
O'Reilly, Matt
O'Reilly, Moira
Orham, Samantha
Oswalt, Yuelle
Oswalt, Hayden

Mozzarella sticks and a DIET Coke.
Look.

Samantha Orham?
I never meet anyone else with my last name...

WAIT!

Uh...

Have a nice day?

You, too?

sigh

MEADVILLE PUBLIC LIBRARY

Man, this library makes St. Francis look like an anthill.
Let's see how much we can find on Samantha Orham.

I need to be back by six thirty, so we'll just have to finish this up tomorrow if that's cool with...
Oh God.

What?

MEADVILLE GAZETTE, Monday, April 5, 2004
Obituaries

Orham, Sam. Age 67 of Meadville and an early advocate for transgender rights, passed away Sunday. He is survived by longtime partner Dina Santiago and one son, James Orham.

I don't think he's your grandmother's lover...

I think he's your grandmother.

Telekinesis is one way to do it, but I found turning the doorknob to be quicker.

Dad...

DAD!

Stop running away! You need to talk to me.

Hey, you two! Mac and cheese with crumble top. What veggie side do you guys—
!
!!

Who told you?
No one told me. Laura and I figured it out.
!!!

Laura?! Wait... Where did you get this?

THE APA

It was me.

I left it for her to find. The check, too.
You said you shredded it!

It came from Sam FOR Amanda. It was her last wish.
No matter what she did to your family, you don't have the right to deny her that!

How dare you go behind my back and...
Her last wish?

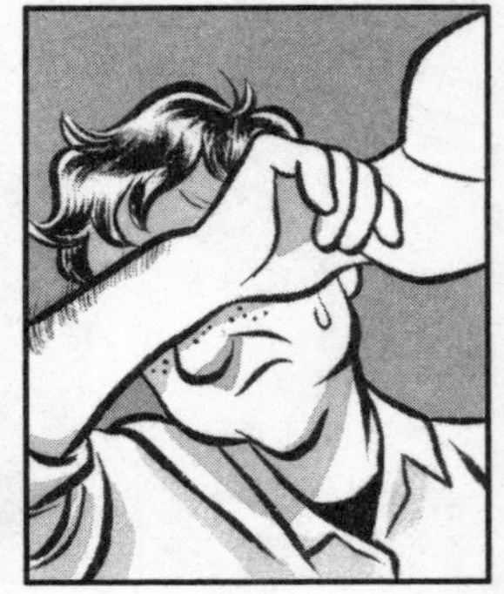

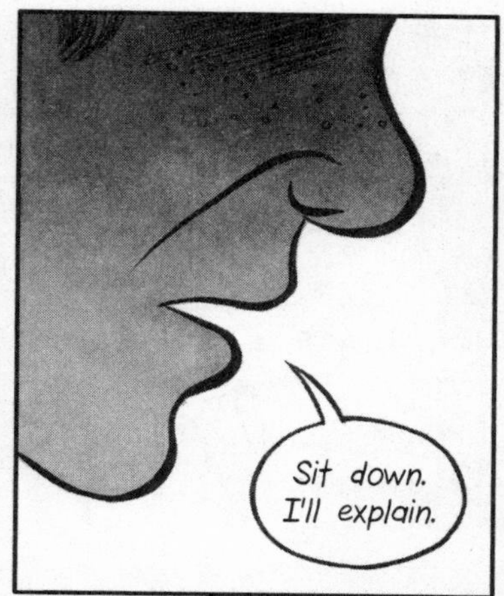
Sit down.
I'll explain.

You, too,
Lucy.
I'm sorry.
I just...

I should
have listened.
Thank
you.

So what do
you know?

Grandma's not
my grandma. My
real grandma
was a man...
She wasn't a MAN.
She was sick.

"Some people just weren't meant to be mothers."

"Some people are selfish and cruel."

"Your real grandmother was twisted. Thank God for my father."

"He saved me."

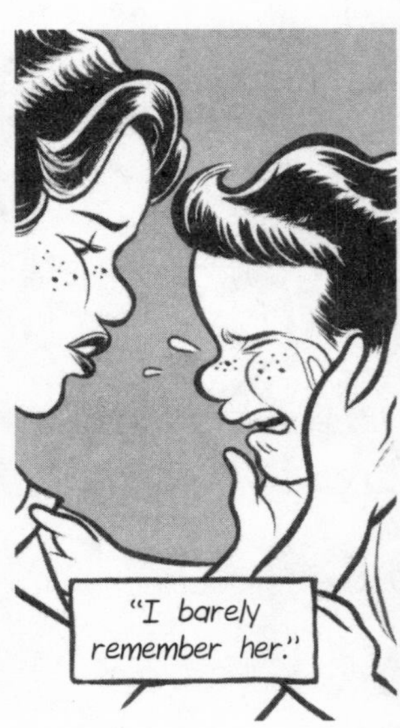
"I barely remember her."

"I do remember one day."
"Came home early from school."

"She was wearing my father's best suit. Fake stubble on her chin, real hairs she had GLUED to her face."

"I was disgusted. I knew then there was something wrong with her, but I had no idea how wrong."

"Until she disappeared."

She left us to live a twisted life with Dina.
Who knows how long she had been cheating. Everyone in town knew, and she didn't try to hide it.

We had to move. Had to start over.
She ruined my childhood.

Oh God. I had no idea.

Dina called last week to beg your dad to attend his mother's funeral.
Bullshit. My mother died a long time ago.

But you went, didn't you?
Why would you go?

Dinner's not going to finish itself. I should probably...
Yeah, of course.

Come here.

Do you understand now? Why I couldn't tell you?
No. You should have told me.

I know you told me not to, but it looks like I accidentally recorded last week's Valley of the Hidden.
I'll get rid of it. Is this the delete button?

click

LAST WEEK ON VALLEY OF THE HIDDEN...

Night, Dad.
I'm sorry...

Shhhh... Nobody likes a groveler.
Groveler? Groveling-er? Maaaan, I gotta sleep.
Sweet dreams, Mads.

And tomorrow, let's go to the bank and deposit that check.
Who cares who sent it? It'll buy a lot of cheese fries.
You can buy ONE frivolous thing, but the rest is going in savings.

Oh...
I kinda already...

Well, I guess the fries are on you this Sunday.

I still can't get over it. It's so crazy!
Tell me about it.
Whoa! Maybe your dad subconsciously misses her? He named you "A MAN. Da."
That's not funny.
And all those pictures of overweight baseball players are not helping at all.

What's going on?
Nothing you don't already know, Detective.

Hey, I found out the craziest thing.
What?
Your grandmother's partner, that Dina? She totally works at the diner we were at the other day!

WHAT?!
Crazy, right? I was Googling them all last night. Here, read this.

I wonder if your grandmother, like, got surgery. Can they even do that? I mean, prosthetic limbs are getting pretty high-tech...
Ew, ew, ew...

Rational numbers are real numbers wit

AMANDA!
Present!
I figured that part out, but I'd like an answer.

Sorry. What was the question?
Put away your love letter and pay attention. See me after class.

She's just bitter she's never gotten laid, never mind gotten a love letter.
At least Sister Clara's dating Jesus.
HA HA ha HA HA ha HA

SAINT FRANCIS
HIGH SCHOOL
I know you were pissed at how bitchy I was to Laura last week, so I made amends.
How so?
SCHOOLBUS

Convinced her and Adam to hang out with us at the show tonight.
Adam? Yeah, no selfish motives behind that.

C'mon, it'll be fun! AND I already asked your parents. They're cool since it's teen night.
Your dad is putty right now. If you ever want a car, ask TODAY.

What about that guy...
K? Get over it. If I let that sort of stuff affect me, I wouldn't go anywhere.
Laura wants you to come!

More accurately, she already thinks you're going and will probably back out if you don't. Soooo, looks like if you want me and her to be friends you have no choice.

The Zipper Presents
TEEN
Gerry!
You remember Amanda?
This is Laura and Adam.
Guys, this is Gerry. His arms are the size of my head!
Hey, man.
Nice to meet you.

You're FRIENDS with that guy?
He's a big teddy bear.

Maybe a teddy bear from a horror film. You know, the kind you put down on the couch, but when you come back it's somehow moved to the chair and is reading a Stephen King book.

You little bitch!
Ho-bag!

No Rick.
Not anymore. He's an idiot.
Hey, I'm Jess. My band goes on third if I can find my crappy lead singer.

This is my brother, Darren.
Hi!
Laura.
Hey, I'm Adam.
Anyone want drinks?

Don't look at me like that! It's teen night. They only serve soda and nasty virgin mixes. Mads, you owe me from last week...
...though I'm SURE you don't remember.

Soda?
Naw! Gimme a virgin!

Anyone else?
I'll take a Coke.
Ditto!
I'll go with you.

This place is insane.
I don't know... I think it grows on—

Crap. It's the same cop-wannabe bartender from the other night.

I knew I shouldn't have come back here.
Don't worry about it. I'll order.

Hey, um...
Can I get three Cokes...
...no, four...
...but one of them is a Diet Coke...
...and a daiquiri.
Virgin.
Virgin daiquiri.

Interesting. So, you're a teenager this week?
Uh.

Chriiis. The sign says "all ages" outside. Are you being a jerk to paying customers again?

Did the math, figured you might need help carrying it all back.
Thanks.
Jess's brother, right?

And you're the one K was pining over. Off the record, I can already tell—you're too good for him.
Or maybe on the record. I don't really care what K thinks.

All right, that's four Cokes (one diet), a daiquiri for TEENAGERS, and a glass of water...
...just in case you also can't handle your nonalcoholic drinks. Hate to have to carry you into a cab.
Again.
$13.

What a jerk!
Eh. I deserve it. But thanks for the help.
Have you seen Jess and K's band yet? I can tell you it's NOT a treat.

Wait... NOT a treat?
Nate! Over here!

Nate, this is Amanda and Laura. Amanda and Laura make up 99 percent of the students of that tiny Catholic School up Route Nine.
Nate goes to Morristown with me and used to totally be in love with K.

In love with K?
That was before we found out K was a douche.
That is, officially, the worst introduction I've ever received.

Just making sure Amanda doesn't make the same mistake.
You're a saint, Darren.
I know.

Uh, I don't have a thing for K.
And I haven't since eighth grade.

Let's start over. I'll do my own introduction. This is Nate, he's a junior at Morristown. He likes music, long walks, and Beaches... the movie. Your turn.
This is Amanda; she's a junior at St. Francis. She likes minor-league baseball, bad movies, and...

...and then he comes home...

...to find his mom dressed up like a man, with, like, REAL HAIR glued to her face!

Cat, shut up.
Seriously, it's not funny.
Hey, Amanda.

Cool that you came to our show.
I didn't realize you guys were playing.

So, Vomit Train REALLY played here?
They are way too big for this place.
They were jerks. You didn't miss anything, Aaron.
Adam.
That's what I said.

I gotta pee.

RESTROOM

So, "Ken'ichi." That's a weird name. What's the origin?
Seattle.

The problem with a best friend who tells great stories was sometimes she didn't know which ones weren't meant for the entire world.

heh hee hee!

HA HA HA HA ha HA ha HA HEE

EXIT

Wasn't into the band.
Liar. I saw you storm out of the bathroom.

Don't let Cat get away with that. There's nothing wrong with transitioning.
Oh yeah. It's TOTALLY normal.

And Cat doesn't mean anything by it.
It doesn't matter if she meant anything by it. She's still being an ass.

I mean, I don't know you that well, so it's not really my place to say, but you need to stop putting that girl on a pedestal.
I love Cat, but she's not always the best person.

This is the kinda crap that happens in high school. It's not forever. The pool of people will get wider and you can be who you want to be.
I mean, the stuff Darren has had to deal with at school...
What the hell does this have to do with Darren?

Oh.

Forget it.
No. Say it.

I just kinda got a vibe and then I saw you staring down Cat when you were kissing K.
It's totally cool if you're queer. You can tell me...
I don't believe this shit.

SLAM!

Goddamn it, Jess. Learn to keep your mouth shut.

I want to go home.

Sorry. We're in the middle of a jam-band set. I can't leave with this crap in my head.
Are you okay?
Um... what just happened?
Where the hell have you been? We're on in five.

Do we need to schedule another band meeting?
Jesus, K, there are only two of us. Any time we talk it's a band meeting. We're having one right now!
I have to go finish that Miller punishment homework.

Besides, I don't really like the crowd here.
I know! These people...
These people don't DANCE.

Don't even pretend like you don't have rhythm, Ms. "Fourth-grade jump rope champion."

Come on!

STOP IT!

I'm cool with leaving.
Lame! Stay for Jess and K's band. That's super shitty if you leave now.
It's also super shitty to tell people I barely know about my grandmother!

Is that why you're upset?! I didn't know. I mean, it's just such a funny story and...
It's not funny to me!

I was wrong. I'm sorry. I...
Adam, you coming?

No, you guys go.
Mads, please don't be mad at me. I didn't think...

I know. I know. I just don't want to talk about it anymore.

So robot cops in the future aren't waterproof? All a criminal has to do is step into a friggin' puddle and the cop shorts out?
POLICE
But you're totally okay with the talking dog?
This is the last time you pick the movie, Sal.

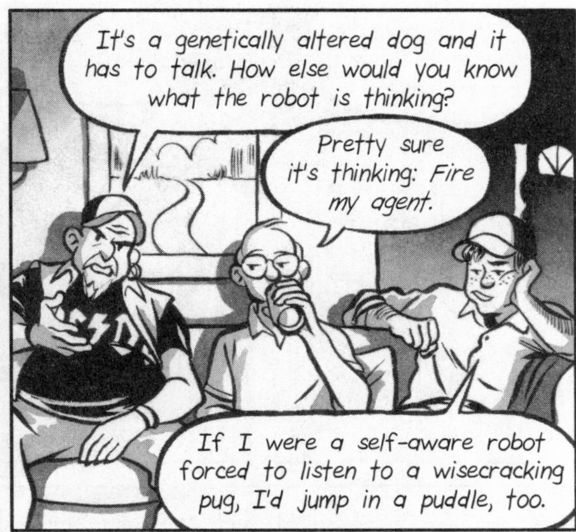
It's a genetically altered dog and it has to talk. How else would you know what the robot is thinking?
Pretty sure it's thinking: *Fire my agent.*
If I were a self-aware robot forced to listen to a wisecracking pug, I'd jump in a puddle, too.

Heeey! If it isn't lady luck!
You're just in time to watch the ending of the worst movie I've ever seen. What's it called? *Robocop and a Half?*

It's RESISTOR 4, and if you watched the others you'd get it's this brilliant metaphor for corruption of the political system...
Good show?

...and how we should be nicer to robots.
Naw. If I want to hear bad music I can just listen to you sing in the shower.
Ahh. Now THERE'S my daughter. Where have you been lately?

Puking on the lawn, I hear.
Hey. None of that.
What? I'm her godfather.

I'm gonna make you an offer you can't refuse...

...someday, and that day may never come...
No more! You win! I'll never drink again!

Good thing, 'cause I'm not sure where to get a horse head.
A head of lettuce would probably work. She's terrified of anything healthy.
Hardy har har.

Laura and Adam come home with you?
Just Laura. Adam stayed for the last band with Cat.

Adam and Cat?
Ugh. I do not like that thought.
As much as I am enjoying this work of art...
I'm telling you, the other three movies were brilliant!

You coming on Sunday?
Wouldn't miss it.
Killed me that you missed Franco opening the other week.

FRANCO WAS A STARTER?!

You're a good kid.
Thanks Dad #2.

I should get to bed.
I appreciate you not staying out late.
I'd hate to be forced to fake-read that book again. Story wasn't that good the last time I fake-read it.

Ever walk into a room you've been in a million times and suddenly it looks completely different?
Like you've never been there before?

FIRST
THE
MEGIMMES
BEST FRIEND
How many times did I go to sleep staring at her face?

AAAH!
Hey, TGIF. Am I right?

I'm not in the mood.
TGIF aka I "Totally Goofed, I'm Fucking Sorry."
Really.

Wouldn't that be TGIFS?
Awww. Fixing my grammar! Friendship returns!

Please just don't tell anyone else.
I won't talk about it again.
Promise.

Luckily, you'll never have to meet your grandma!
I kinda feel bad about that. I woulda liked to meet him.
Haha! Yeah, "him."

Ugh, you are so smart for leaving early last night.
I mean, Jess is one of my favorite people and all, but holy crap, does their band blooow.

Any progress with "Operation Incest"?
You kidding me? Adam friggin' PINES for you. It's bordering on pathetic. Almost enough to deter me.

Almost.
Hey, you still have to do the soup kitchen tomorrow?

Yup. Me and Killer Miller are gonna be BFFs in no time.
Awesome! I'll join you.

Wow, I think I need a Q-tip. I almost thought you said you wanted to work the soup kitchen. You know, the only guys there are fifty and mostly toothless.
I mean, I know you aren't very picky, but...
Ha. Ha.

I feel bad about last night...and the day before...and, hell, I probably did something dumb the day before that.
I owe it to you. I could use a Karma cleaning.

I'm not sure volunteering in a Catholic church helps with Karma.
Jesus wants us all to glow blue.

What time should I pick you up?
My dad's gonna work, too. You mind driving with him?

By "driving" you mean he's going to belt the Monkees and swerve back and forth to "dance"?
Pretty sure that's the only way he knows how to operate a vehicle.

"I-I-I-I-I'm not your..."

"...stepping-stone..."

HA HA HA
Don't encourage him!

Amanda! So good of you to come.
Cat, oh, this is a surprise. Glad to have the extra hands!
Hi, Father Tim.

Shouldn't be too busy today. Nice spring days are always quiet. Thank the Lord.
I know teenagers are never here voluntarily, so I want to say we appreciate you helping out no matter the reason behind it.

"The way to the Lord's heart is through putting mashed potatoes in other people's stomachs."
heh heh

Morning, girls!

Just to warn you, Amanda's, like, the worst cook in history. Her mom won't let her within ten feet of a stove.
Cat's not kidding.

We all have our talents. Luckily, Sara's talent is seasoning. We're known for our mashed potatoes, and I can assure you it's not from the quality of the potatoes.

Thanks again, girls. She'll be along to pick up a batch soon.
GRADE D

Which way does this thing go?
Er. Up and down?

Whoops.
Remind me not to eat any of this.

What are these? Like, mutant potatoes?

Dammit! This is impossible.

At least they bounce.
Aw, crap.
Catherine, it would be good for you to remember you're in a church.

Of course, Ms. Miller.
We came to pick up the first batch.
Though it looks like you two need a little more time.

May I borrow that?

Note to self: Avoid knifefights with nuns.
You might want to spend less time talking and more time thinking why you're here.
They'll get the hang of it, Sara. Thanks for helping, girls.

Sara?
I would have never guessed that was her first name. It sounds so...
...sweet.

Woo! I DID IT!
You need to get out more.

My grandparents get back from the cruise today. They're coming over for dinner.
Oh man, you gonna confront them?

I can't decide.

How do you tell someone: "Hey, I know you aren't my real grandma! Thanks for lying all these years!"
Besides, my dad made some big promise to keep silent or something.

Kids shouldn't have to make those kinda promises. Then again, kids shouldn't have to deal with having two dads.
Jesus had two dads.

You keep talking.
I guarantee you "Sara" would love to hear all about it.

Hee hee. "Jesus had two dads."
Hey! You excited about the fireman's fair?

When is it?
Wow, it's not like you to forget a date with fried dough.

Mmm, fried dough.
Next weekend. I'm not sure if I'm going. Not a big fan of rides assembled in less time than I brush my teeth.

I've got three more weeks of potatoes. But I totally want to go to the fair at night.
And the aaaaafter-party?

Have you thought more about what you're going to do with the money?
Yup. Manatee. Just trying to find a large enough tank.

You're such a weirdo.

Not bad.

I can't believe we just got a compliment out of Killer Miller.
I can't believe you're taking any credit for it! What are you on, potato number four?

No way! I peeled like...

...um...four.

BUT the one that dropped and broke in half should totally count as two.

Last one! Want to peel it together?
Yeeeah, no. I don't trust you with that thing.

But it's like a symbol of our friendship! We can make it into best-friend charms.
Or matching spud earrings!
Ooh, or get it taxidermied in an action pose! Can you carve it some legs?
Haha. I love you, Amanda Orham!

Done! I feel like my arms are going to fall off.

I can assure you they won't. Catherine, follow me to the kitchen for dishwashing. Amanda, start on those carrots.

"I love you, Amanda Orham."

To quote the classic film E.T., "Oooooch."

Am I going to wake up really buff tomorrow?
If you'd come to my classes, you might not be in so much pain now.

I'm totally in shape!
You're thin. Not strong. There's a difference.

Stop with the cookies! They'll be here in fifteen minutes.
I have a separate cookie stomach.

I thought we agreed to dress for dinner?
I did.

I was really hoping you would wear something a little more...
A little more what?
What ever happened to that nice blue dress?

My matching giant hair bow was in the wash.
Watch your tone. Just go and put it on.

Now.

DING DONG

Ack! They're early. They're ALWAYS early, but this is early even for them.
Quick, put these on the table.

Use the hotplates!

Mom! Dad!
Great to see you.

We don't appreciate prank calls.

Um...okay?
We have caller ID. Leave a message next time.
Where is she?

Hi.
There she is!

How was Alaska?

And cue the passive-aggressive comments on how I look...

You're so pretty. Why are you always hiding it? Next weekend we're going shopping.

I actually have plans.

Good to know she's reliable...even if she isn't my real grandma.

Was it one of those cruises that folds your towels into animals?
A sweaty immigrant putting their hands all over my towel? No thank you.
We had them stop after the first day, but it was an elephant.

One more minute.
Amanda, any news to tell?

Sit down, Jim. Lucy's perfectly capable.
Starting to think about colleges more.

I might go to State to save money. I can always go to a good grad school after.
Any new steady? Anyone special your grandfather and I should know about?

HA.

I don't appreciate whatever you're laughing about.
The boys Amanda dates are lucky if they get a second date. Not exactly the definition of "steady."
There's no one I'm interested in.
Lots of nice Catholic boys at that school. I didn't raise my granddaughter to be a snob. You know, I was practically married when I was your age—so was your dad.

Dad, quit it. Amanda's too young!
We couldn't even drink at our wedding. We toasted our future with sparkling grape juice.
There. All ready.

So, you two were married at eighteen?

You know, I don't think I've ever seen your wedding pictures. I'm sure you looked gorgeous, Grandma.

Why, thank you, dear. Unfortunately the album was destroyed in that basement flood. But enough about that.
You must have given them out to friends? Someone must have one. I can scan it and print up some new ones for you.
Amanda, can I talk with you in the kitchen?

Are you going to do this all night?
Do what?
Try to force your grandparents into telling you about Sam?
Oh, that. Yes. That was my plan.
Amanda, I promised I wouldn't tell you. My father is not a forgiving man. Talking to him about it won't change the past, but can make our lives harder in the future. Do you understand?

You know, Dad, you've actually made things more clear. I'll do the right thing.

That's my girl.

I know about Sam, and I know you're lying.

How dare you...
Dad, wait.
JAMES DAVID ORHAM. Kitchen! Now!

NO!
He had nothing to do with this. I figured it out on my own.

Stop pretending! I just want to know what happened.
I need to use the little girls' room.

You'll be an adult when you start acting and dressing like one.

You want to follow in your disgusting grandmother's footsteps? Because I will NOT have a sinner for a granddaughter.

Light or dark.
Light, please.

Amanda, light or dark?

Can I have a leg?

PLOP

Say grace, James.

Bless us, O Lord—
—for these Thy gifts—
—which we are about to receive from Thy bounty.
Through Christ our Lord.
Amen.
Amen.
Amen.

Thanks for a lovely dinner. I'm sure it was delicious before we had to microwave it.
Thank you, Mom.
Remember what I said.
I know. I will.

Come here, you.

I know I'm not your biological grandmother, but I love you. I wish we had told you ourselves.
It's so cold out here! You'd never know it was spring.

Next time you come over, take River Road. Five minutes faster.
I hate River Road. It's overrun with deer.
I didn't say there weren't deer. I said it was faster.
If you pay attention, you can easily avoid them.

Just.
Don't.

Nice dress.

Nice dress.

N-i-c-e d-r-e-s-s.

Rain? Wonderful.
Jim, we just left mass. No complaining.

Game's off.
Dammit.
Jim!
Hey, nice dress. I don't know if I've ever seen you in one.
If everyone keeps making it such a big deal, it'll be the last time, too.

Don't be an idiot, Adam.
I was just trying to say she looked nice.
If the game's canceled, I could use Amanda's help at Large Buys.

Okay with you?
What? Sure.

Fresh Rain or Vanilla Wildflower?
Wild Vanilla Rain.

I like that one, too.

My insides still felt like pulp.
Mushed paper, ink illegible, dissolving together.

BZZZZT.
Amanda Orham, please report to the principal's office.
Oooooh!

Have you been having fun without me?

PRINC

Grandma?

Thought I would take my favorite granddaughter out to lunch. We never get any time alone.
Um. Okay.

HAPPY HANK'S
Of all the restaurants I expected her to turn into... this was not on the list.

BRO
Have you never been here before?
Oh my.
Well, no. But I thought you'd like it.
Please Wait to Be Seated

Welcome to Happy Hank's, where the smiles are free and the meals practically are, too! Just you guys?
Yes. Two. Not by the kitchen.
All righty!

Try Our New
Chili Cheese Fart Fries!
You Won't Regret it
But Your Friends Might!

Is that sword secure?
He only kills good guys, so as long as you eat sinfully you should be fine.
Haha.

We can go somewhere else. Where do you usually like to eat lunch?

NO! I mean... I'm just not in the mood to bump into anyone. No distractions, just you and me.

Okay.

So...

...you go see any good Broadway shows late—
I should have done something about the way Sam was. I had no choice but to marry your grandfather and lie to you!
She was diseased and she is burning in hell and it's all my fault!

I'll give you another minute.

I was being stupid the other night. You're my grandma. You're the one who came to my spelling bees. You're the one who comes over on Christmas. You've been there for me. I don't care what I found out.

Samantha was a wonderful woman.

She was my best friend. When I kissed her, I had no idea what it would do to her!
...

More time? Okay! GREAT!

You're gay?!?!
AMANDA, watch your mouth. How could you even think for a second...

"But you just said..."
"We were twelve. I had a crush on Kenny Samson down the street—adorable boy with fiery red hair."
"He went into the service. Died. Would have probably married him if—"

"Grandma!"

"How was I supposed to learn how to kiss? And Samantha really was the one who started it."
"It was practice for me, nothing more."

But it unleashed some demon in her. Jumbled her mind. When we were seventeen, she tried to tell me she was "not a woman." Can you believe that? She thought she was a man! Have you ever heard anything so ridiculous?!
There's a lot of people who feel that way. I was read—

Now, I was a good friend. I didn't shun her or make fun of her... I did avoid her for a few weeks, but I needed time to think. I needed to HELP her.

I couldn't help how I looked. People were always asking if I was a model. I should never have used her for practice.
Girlfriends did that sort of thing. I'm sure you practiced on a friend when you were young.

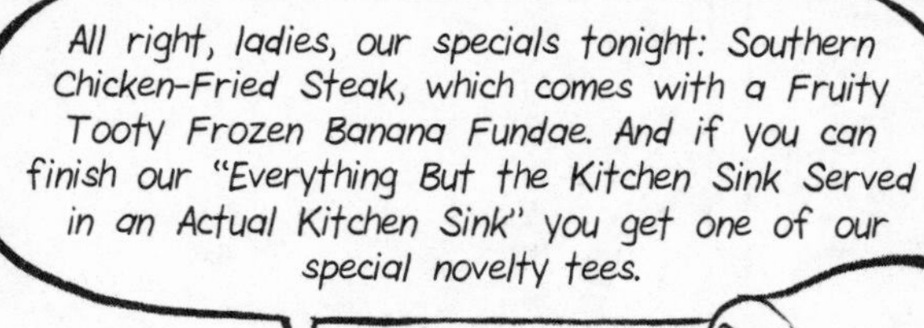

Where were we...

You were about
to say something
super shitty.

Watch your language.
See? For ONE thing,
there's your tendency
to swear. It's not as
light a sin as your
generation thinks!

Your father, bless his heart, didn't do a great job raising you. The baseball, the action movies, the slacks...
...and I've never once seen you with makeup on. He should know better.

What?
What he didn't do is teach you how to be a lady. I'm not sure where your mother failed. Androgyny is a dangerous line to walk. The devil could easily pull you to one side or the other.

People aren't born gay; but some people ARE born weak. It's like not having a strong immune system. The slightest germ could cause an infection.
This is ridiculous.

"I loved your grandmother. Not in the way she wanted, but when she went crazy and left, I stepped in and cared for your father and your grandfather."

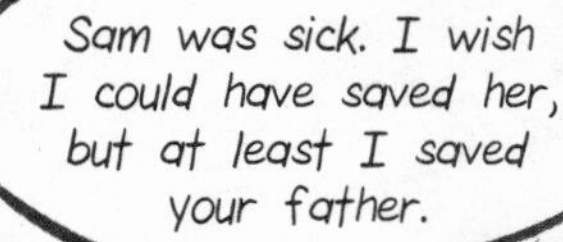
Sam was sick. I wish I could have saved her, but at least I saved your father.

Where is our food? The service here is horrible!
I really need to get back to school.

Waiter! We'll take the check.

Um...you didn't order anything.
Oh.

SAINT FRANCIS CATHOLIC HIGH SCHOOL

I'm so glad we had this conversation.
Please just promise me you'll be careful.
Also, I'd rather you not tell your parents about us meeting.

Anything interesting happen at school today?
No.

tikka
tac
takka

Boogle
How to tell if you are
tikkety
tik
tak

BING!
Chat with laurapage3
urapage3: Hey!
adVOTH: gay
Ahh!

laurapage3: Huh? Who's gay?
MadVOTH: haha sorry fingers on the wrong keys.

laurapage3: Oh. What are you up to?
BING!
Chat with Hojo86
Hojo86: guess who finally got his own computer. i'll give you a hint it starts with an "m" and ends with an "e."
Reply

MadVOTH: i was just talking with your sister.
Hojo86: good tell her to put on shoes. her feet stink.

MadVOTH: your brother got his own computer?
laurapage3: Unfortunately yes. And he won't stop rubbing it in.
laurapage3: Granted he bought it with his own money so I can't really complain. But still, so annoying.

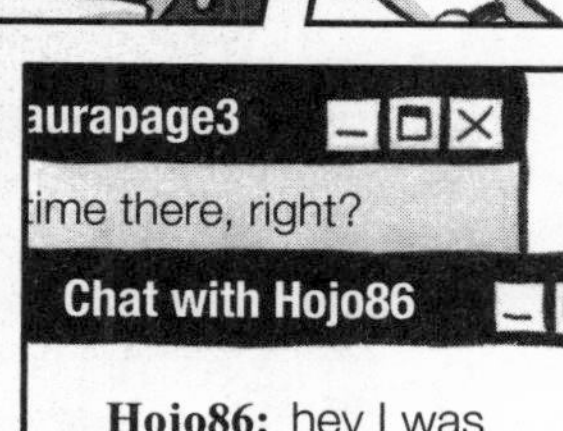
laurapage3: Hey, I know Cat kept you company last week so I figured it was my turn. Want me to volunteer at the kitchen next weekend? You still doing time there, right?

BING!
tikka taka tik

ENTER
SHIFT

aurapage3
time there, right?
Chat with Hojo86
Hojo86: hey I was wondering if you wanted to go to the fireman's fair together Sat night? my treat of course.
MadVOTH: that would be awesome. you're the best!

Chat with laurapage3

Want me to volunteer at the kitchen next weekend? You still doing time there, right?

oh no! i just tried to respond to you but hit the wrong tab! i think i accidentally said yes to a date with adam. arr

Send

BUZZZ

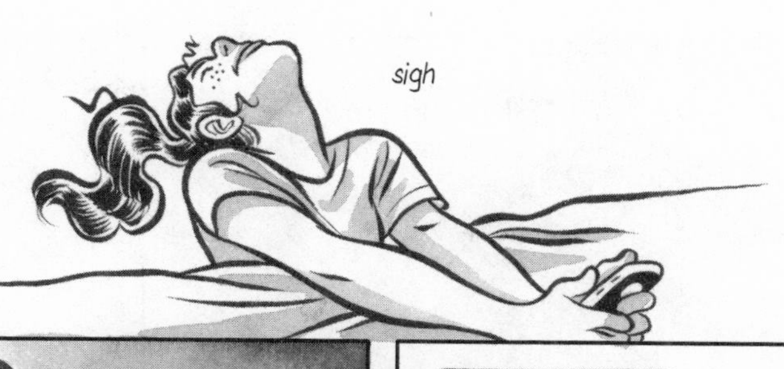
sigh

Chat with Hojo86
Hojo86: great! we could go out to dinner before if you aren't into fair food and if the fair sucks we can just skip it and watch a movie. i've wanted to see OCEAN'S 47 for a while and i hear COVER YOUR EYES is really awesome if you go for scary movies. it's got that actor that always looks a little constipated. what's his name? adrian something?

MadVOTH: sorry i gotta run.

MadVOTH: crap. long story, but make sure you don't make plans on sat night. You might have to save me from a date with your brother. talk later.

Since when do you smoke?
I don't. I'm just getting rid of these so my mom will stop.

So, what's up?
Got in a fight with Jess.

About what?
Let's just say she's a crazy bitch who likes spreading rumors.

What was she saying?

It doesn't matter.

You'd tell me if you had some big secret, right?
I mean, sure, but I don't have any.

I shouldn't have to deal with this sort of shit at the Zipper. It was my place before it was hers.

It was getting lame anyway. All those Public kids and their fake IDs. I gotta find a new hangout. You ever been to Transit?
You know I haven't.

Saturday let's go. Haven't heard of any of the bands, but maybe one won't suck.
Are you forgetting about the fireman's fair?
I'm really not in the mood.

Well...don't be mad, but I think I accidentally agreed to go to the fair with Adam.
On a date.

Please don't be pissed! I know you like him.

It's about damn time! I'm totally cool with you going out with Adam, but promise me one thing.
Of course. Anything.

Stop being such a prude.

These things taste like crap.

Thanks for cheering me up. Night, Mads.

Oh no.
Amanda Lynn Orham...

...I challenge you to a game of Dragons and Daggers!

You're on!

PLAYER 2, CHOOSE YOUR DRAGON.
P1
P2

You're seriously choosing Inkblood? She's got the lowest firepower. Not Basilbreath?
DING!
I'm always Basilbreath. Besides, thought I would go easy on you, mortal. Remind me again how many times I've beaten you at this?

ARG! HA! HUT. HUT! YAAA! FOOOOOOM.
AAAAAAAH. DRAGON WINS.
Hmm... seven out of thirteen?
Naw. I like to stay in my species.
Okay, but don't start crying when I BBQ your butt again.
Want to be a dragon, too, this time?

Have you ever played as the villagers?
Why would I want to do that when I can do this...?
FOOOOOM. AAAAH. DRAGON WINS.

So, are you seriously not going to mention the fact I just snuck in way after curfew?
Nope!

All right, who are you, what have you done with my dad, and how did you learn to play Dragons and Daggers as badly as him? CONFESS!

I haven't been a good dad lately or a good friend...
Hell, I've been a pretty lousy human being. I hate knowing I put you through so much.

I'm not worried about what you're up to. I'm just glad things are starting to go back to normal between us.
Normal...

Even if normal means me getting burned to a crisp.
DRAGON WINS.
If your villager friends would stop poking me with pitchforks I'd stop my *Fahrenheit 451* reenactment and listen to your sappy speech.
You're my best friend. You know that, right?
DRAGON WINS.
Heeeey!

This seemed a lot more fun in my imagination.

I tried to warn you! Cat made it pretty entertaining, though.

Amanda, your ride is here.
He's totally early. Big surprise.

You ready?!

Geez.
Bet you didn't think someone could get this sweaty peeling carrots.

Actually, I was just averting my eyes from your glowing halo. That thing is blinding, Saint Amanda!
You're such a kiss-up.

But if you want to stop by your house and shower, that's cool with me. I don't mind waiting.
Thanks. I feel like an oil-spill duck.

Be good, Adam.

SSSSSSSSSSSHHHHHHHHHHHH
It's just a date.
Just a date.

SSSSSSHHHH

SSSSSS...CLICK
rnadoes Fan Club
1

Lovely. I'm a perfect rectangle.

Okay, which of these say, "I've never had any gay thoughts about my best friend"?
If you're having trouble deciding, go with sequins.

This shirt is trying way too hard.
Just adjusting my hoopskirt.

You look beautiful.

Ow. Hey!
Hush your mouth. Let's go.

IREMAN'S FAIR

This is the first year I've ever been here without Cat.
Her loss!

I got you a necklace. Those are real rubies. If you resell it on eBay, I'll be pissed.
So, what's first?

Hmmm. Gravitron or Teacups?
Ah, yes. Spinning until we vomit. My favorite as well.

GRAVITRON

Come on! Just try.
Like this?

Eeeeee.
Haha!

Eeeeee.
HAHA!

Show-off.
THUMP!

PRET
FUNNEL CAKE
I'm pretty sure there are more deep-fried things. You can't give up now.
I'm going to diiiie.

Hey!
Hey! I thought you weren't coming?
I wouldn't hug her too tight.

Aw, you get one, too.

You hear about the bonfire at Jon's? You guys have to come.
Definitely! We can make s'mores. Mmm, foooood...
It won't be so funny when I puke on your sneakers.

I would never wash them again.
Ewwww!
Yeah, "ewwww" is right. Get a room, you two.

You know I'm not into parties.
Hey, promises! No prude-ing!

Fine.
Woo!

BING
Just sent the address.
Hey, I'm—

See you later!

Poor guy.
Eh. I think he'll be happy by the end of the night.

She's not a slut, you know.
Sorry, I didn't mean...

Hey, are you sure you're cool with going to the party? I mean, I've never seen you at one.

It's not a party. It's a BONFIRE, where I assume we eat bonbons and set things on fire. Right?
Exactly.

To: Laura Page
please please come
to this party! Can't
find Cat. so. BORED.

HA HA HA HA
PHUP PHUP
PHUPP PHBB
BUZZZ

Laura
Sorry. No way I'm
hanging with that
crowd. You fending
Adam off okay?
Reply
Options

he keeps trying to hold
my hand and i keep
pretending my nose is
itchy. if i started picking
it would that drive him
away or make him want
me more?

There you are!
BUZZZ

Mads. You're at a PARTY!
FINALLY!
Haha.

GLUG
GLUG

Hey, Page. Get that ass inside and get your date another beer!

Sure thing. You need one, Cat?
Hell no!
I need TWO!
Yeah, I think she's had enough.

HA HA HA HA HA HA

Sooooo???
So what?
Did you guys make a baby yet?! I'm getting impatient!

It's not going to happen, Cat. I just can't think of Adam that way!

Listen, I wasn't going to tell you this, but you have to stop being so cold. People are saying things, and you're not helping.
What are you talking about?

People have this ridiculous idea that you have some sort of crush on me.
Haha.

This is where you're supposed to get angry and deny it.

I know, but...
Oh God. I think I'm going to be sick.

It's...

...true.

K, you seen Cat?
Oh, hey, Amanda.

Wait, Amanda? No way. THAT'S the dyke?
Shut up, man.
Cat just went into one of the bedrooms with Rick.
Wait. What?

Don't mind K. He's an idiot. Me, I got nothing against lesbians. Actually, I'm a big lesbian fan.
I said, shut the fuck up!

He's just upset he turned a perfectly good girl gay.
Eyes all around, drilling into whatever shield I used to have.

What the hell is wrong with you guys?
Amanda!

Whoa!
Hey there, speed racer.

Wait. What happened?
Listen, Amanda, if it's true, I'm cool with it, and—

KISS NUMBER 7
If it's a line...
...and the slightest thing could pull me to one side or the other...
...I want this side...
I need this side.

...and...uh...
Oh, shit.

Want to explore the house?

You have no idea how long I've wanted to kiss you.

We don't need to rush. I want to enjoy it...

Please.

I really want to.
It's just...
I've never...

It's okay. Me neither.

But— I'm not... No— let's wait.
I don't want to wait.

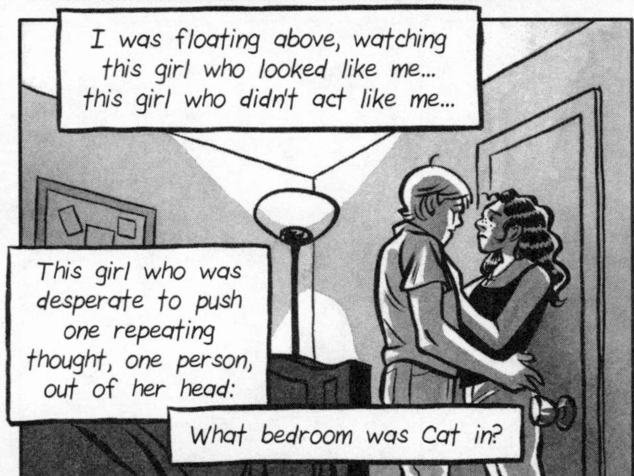
I was floating above, watching this girl who looked like me... this girl who didn't act like me...
This girl who was desperate to push one repeating thought, one person, out of her head:
What bedroom was Cat in?

I'm so crazy about you, Mads.
There is a line. Grandma was right. And I was born on the wrong side of it.
Oh God. Please forgive me.

I have to use the bathroom.

Oh, of course, sure.

The worst part is, I was more upset that Cat was in another bedroom.

Tell me.
I don't want to talk about it.

Did Adam do something? I swear I'll kill him if he—
No. It's just...
Cat ditched me and... I did something dumb. I really don't want to talk about it.

Seriously, if Adam was a jerk—
No. He was fine. It's Cat. She just...I can't really talk about it.

Listen, I don't want to preach, but I need to get this off my chest.
You have to stop letting Cat have so much control over you.

You know Cat doesn't care about anyone but herself.
Laura's mouth kept moving, but I didn't hear the words. I just heard the name.

Cat.

...and she'll never...

KISS NUMBER 8

Cat...

Listen, I—
Get. Out.

Laura, I didn't mean—
I SAID GET OUT! GET OUT!

VROOOOM

Up. Up. We're going to be late for church.

I woke up in a fog, but looking back I realize it wasn't fog.
It was gas.
Flammable.
Waiting for a spark.
JIM! Time to go.

Guess it's just you and me. Your dad has work.
I'm not feeling so great. Can I just stay home?

You look horrible. Amanda...were you drinking again?
I just had trouble sleeping.

I hope you're not coming down with something.
Actually, I got in a fight with Laura and Cat... well, and Adam. I really can't face them all today.

Take this and put your shoes on. Fighting with your friends is part of growing up.

I could have pushed harder, gotten Mom to let me stay home.
But maybe I wanted to be judged.
Maybe I knew the scale of 1 to 10 didn't even come close to being able to rank what I had done.

sigh

Good morning, Mrs. Stevenson.
Humff.
SAINT FRANCIS

Laura, look at me. Look at me.

Oh, Mark! Over here. Would you mind giving Amanda a lift to the game? Jim can't make it.

I'm not going.
I can't believe one of you guys would EVER miss a game. It must be something very impor—

That was odd.

Sorry, hon. I would drive you, but I've got to get to work.
It's okay. I don't really feel up for it today.

I could smell the sulfur of the match. The fire was coming.

Sorry I didn't call yesterday. I was too hungover to move and lost my stupid charger.
Sooooo...what happened? K said he saw you guys making out and going upstairs!
Listen, about what you asked me—

I was so drunk. I barely remember talking to you at all!
Sooo! Tell me everything!

Did you guys... well, you know?!

Laura's gonna freak!

Speaking of which, where the hell is she? Has she EVER been late?

There's something —
BRRRRRRIIIING

So, Friday night. Transit? Yes?

BRRRRRRRRRRRRRIIIIIIIIIIINNNG
PLOP

RRRRIP

I'm SO sorry. We need to talk.

YOINK!

Principal's office. NOW.

Beautiful red apples losing color. A small dot of mold appears.

SLAM

Growing with a pulsating life as the apple below it collapses from the inside out.

The mold starts to shake, to move, and soon it's spreading like a wave taking over the shore.

EM

Wait.

Tell me it's not true. You better fucking tell me it's not true.

Whatever it is you've heard...
Yeah, it's probably true.

Goddamn it, Mads! How could you lie to me?! All these years?
I never lied!

You just happened to keep "forgetting" to tell me you like to throw yourself on women?
Who told you that?

The whole school is talking about it. How you used Adam and attacked Laura—
It wasn't that way!
That's not what Laura says.

I've been going around like an IDIOT for months defending you...
...swearing to people you "aren't gay, you're just picky."
You should have just told me!
I only kissed Laura because I needed to make sure!
Oh, I'm sure you would have loved to find out I've had a crush on you for years!

EXIT
ONL

EXIT

EXIT
ONLY
click

Shit.

Uh...It's lunch break. I forgot a notebook and came home to—
Bad day?

Yeah.

Well, I think you could use a day off. A Lifetime movie is about to start. I know you don't like them, but—
That would be awesome.

Even made some popcorn. Bought the REAL kind for once. Extra butter. Shhh, don't tell my boss.
Air-conditioning broke again at work so I took the afternoon off.
Thanks.

Considering you're such a bad-movie lover, I'm very surprised you haven't embraced THESE movies by now.
YASMINE BLEETH HAS A FACE TO DIE FOR.

I always assumed they were love stories.
Women setting houses on fire is more fun than happy endings.
I LOVE YOU! I DON'T CARE AT ALL THAT YOUR FACE IS HORRIBLY DISFIGURED.
NOW...UM...CAN YOU ROB THIS OLD MAN FOR ME? I MEAN, I WOULD, BUT I'M REALLY BUSY...

Hey, Mom. There's something I need to tell you.

I think I might be gay.
I know, honey.
I know.

What...
How did you know?

Your father saw you the other night.
With Laura.
He was... upset.
Oh, God.

Listen...

You're my daughter, and I love you. I think I've always known.
My gut says God is okay with it, too.
And Dad...

He'll come around.

He saw. I can't believe he saw.
Ooh, this is the best part!
YOU GAVE ME PLASTIC SURGERY TO LOOK EXACTLY LIKE YOUR DEAD WIFE?!
DID I? MY BAD.

The next month
was a blur.

When you're a teenager,
you think that adults aren't
susceptible to gossip.

That it doesn't cloud the way they act.
That somehow petty cruelty is a thing
you outgrow like a pair of jeans.
Stop it.

PRINCIPAL

It doesn't help when almost every person you've ever cared about avoids you.

LAST WEEK ON
VALLEY OF THE HIDDEN.

Not everyone was horrible to me.

A-

Nice job, Amanda.

It's just really hard to remember the nice parts.

One: I finally got my mom to start going to Tornadoes games, since Dad, Mark, and Adam wouldn't come anymore, and that'd be a lot of season tickets wasted.

Two: The Tornadoes have been doing amazing lately. Sal's convinced Dad was bad luck.

The thing that haunted me most wasn't the name-calling, or the loneliness, or Cat.

...and knowing she kissed me back.

No! She's our daughter. You can't just put on blinders. If you don't come home in the next half hour...
No, I'm not! How could you— gah!
click

Mom?
Amanda, we need to talk.

I keep trying to pretend it's going to get better, but...
It's okay. I'm getting used to it.

No!
I don't want you to ever "get used to it." No one should treat you the way your father has—or your so-called friends!

Now, don't get mad, but I have an idea. If you hate it, forget I ever brought it up.

I know you only have a month left in the year...but I think it might be best if you transfer to Public. I know it'll be horrible not knowing anyone, and—

Oof.

I guess that's a yes?

Okay, God. These might be the gates of heaven.
I have a choice to make. I can put my invisibility cloak back on and act like I'm not constantly thinking about kissing my female friends.
MORRISTOWN HIGH SCHOOL
Or I can just be myself, and tell people, "Hey, I'm Amanda! And I happen to be gay!" Maybe even reverse it. "Hey, I'm gay! And I happen to be Amanda!"
If you feel like tossing me any advice...

Watch it!
Oof.

Advice received: Stop inner-monologuing in crowded entryways.

beeeep

Hurry it up! You're making everyone late!

Heaven was a bit more stressful than I expected.

Room 207...207...
It's gotta be on the second floor, right?

312
Floor 2
What the hell?! 312? Who teaches math here?
You lost, little girl?

Oh, thank God! Nate, right? Likes music and *Beaches*, the movie.
Even music from *Beaches*, the movie.
Pretty sure St. Francis isn't on the second floor.

I transferred. It's—it's a long story.
Haven't seen you at the Zipper in a while.
That's also a long story.
How can you be so tiny and so full of long stories?

Listen, I should go.
207's on the north side.

Oh, thanks.

You have no idea which direction north is, do you?
Of course I do.

Up?

Come on, I'll show you.
Won't you be late?
Naw. I got an honor society pass.

Whoa. Those actually exist? I thought I made them up.
Huh?
Never mind.

Faggot.
Says the guy who showers naked with thirty other boys every day.

Yeah, and you're jealous.
Dude, that sounded kinda gay.
"Faggot" is so overplayed. I wish they'd try to branch out—wood pun intended. Maybe "unicorn rider" or "bear trap."
I've also always been a fan of the British "poof." I mean, who wouldn't want to sound like a magic spell?

Do you get picked on a lot?
Sure, but luckily there's a lot of us, and we have a pretty kick-ass Gay-Straight Alliance. And yes, I am mostly saying that because I'm the vice president.

I think you'll help, though.
Help with what?
Balancing out the ratio of crappy human beings. This place is too damn small.

You're kidding. Aren't there, like, two thousand students?
I know all these people, and I'm sick of ALL of them. From kindergarten to junior year...hell, I know their blood types by heart.

See that guy?
O-positive. And that one: B-negative.
And THAT one: no blood. Cyborg.

There you are. Room 207.
Thank you so much. If I hadn't run into you, they'd have found me balled up in the fetal position in the middle of the hallway.
207

So, you agree you owe me one? Because you do.
Sure.
Come to the Zipper tonight. My new band is playing. We have negative-three fans so far.

I don't know. I don't exactly have many friends...
Exactly the reason you should kiss up to me. I'm prime friend material.
Come. Or else I'll never tell which way south is.

Down!
Darn, you're too smart for me.

The Zipper? Isn't that Cat's hangout?
Not anymore.

Are any of your friends going?

I don't think it's a good idea. I know you're tough and can take the verbal abuse, but it's just not safe. Also, you don't exactly have a great record of making the right choices in that setting.
Mom, I'll be fine.

Friends? Wait, I vaguely remember what those are.
Sorry. Forget I said that. Mom reflex.

I'm sorry, but my answer is no.
Oh, come on!

What's going on?

Amanda wants to go to the Zipper, but it's a bad idea. It's a school night, and she doesn't really know anyone else going and—
—I haven't done anything fun in a month. Some new kids from Public invited me.

So let her go.

It's cool, Mom. I'll be okay.

Nice of you to pick NOW to start talking to your daughter again.
Had to happen sometime.

ZIPPERS
Hey, Gerry.

Amanda! You totally came!
Yeah.

I'm so glad, 'cause Nate's ex is here and you'll totally distract him. I HATE her. Like, HATE in all caps.
Wait... "her"?

Yeah, "her." Nate doesn't discriminate. He crushes on horrible people of all types.

Are Jess and K playing tonight, too?
K? K is so old news.

He freaked when they got a bad review and blamed it all on Jess. Crazy, considering the reviewer loved her but said his falsetto sounded like a goat and a chihuahua having sex.

Ha! They really said that?
Well, no, but they should have.

This is awesome. Morristown could use more smart, queer folk.
You better join the GSA. I'm president this year. I let Nate be VP even though he's USELESS.

Thanks, but no thanks.

Don't tell me you're seriously considering going back in the closet when half of your body is already out?

Oh well. Can't say I didn't try to include you.

Dad was right. Always choose flying over invisibility.
When's the next meeting?

Err...hello?

We're, uh...
Well, I guess we don't have a name yet. This is our first show.
If I crap my pants, I'm sorry.
Actually, it would be cool if you all close your eyes or, you know, turn around.
Definitely cover your ears.
Maybe go to the convenience store across the street for a half hour until we're done. Have a plate of nachos or one of those sweaty rotary hot dogs.
Or, you know, you could just stay and...

...ROCK THE FUCK OUT!

Hi, new girl.
You guys were amazing!

Naw. But we'll get there.
Speak for yourself! I agree with Darren.

Nate told me you were coming. I didn't think you'd show.
I'm sorry.
You must hate me. I don't know why I was acting like some kind of fucking expert on human emotions.

I want you to know I didn't say anything to Cat. I didn't start the rumors.
Well, I didn't MEAN to.

K wouldn't shut up about you...and to try to get him to shut up I stupidly suggested that maybe you weren't interested in boys at all. I had no idea he'd go straight to Cat and start this whole horrible thing.
It's not a horrible thing.

You helped me know who I am a little bit more, or something Hallmark-ish like that.

Then that makes two good things that came out of this mess!
Two?

You probably noticed I don't play with K anymore.

Hey, do you guys like mozzarella sticks?

Am I seriously taking my new friends to meet my dead grandma's lesbian lover?

And follow-up question: I'm finally out of the closet, so why can't I stop looking at the new boy who likes boys?

Hey, kids. Welcome back. Just the four?
Dina?

I wish. She's over there.
snort

DINA

Amanda.
DINA

How did you know it was me?
As a grandmother—well, step-grandmother— it's a requirement to obsessively follow whatever your grandkids do.
The internet was a godsend. We loved your blog. Sad when you stopped updating. We still follow your photo stream.
I mean I... Sam did. But he's gone.
Oh God. I'm rambling. I'm just really happy right now.

clink
clink

Why didn't you contact me?
Sam tried to contact your dad. A few times. It...

...It didn't go well.

What kills me the most is your dad still thinks Sam abandoned him.
What do you mean?

People rarely remember the past the way it happened. Most remember... however it suits their needs.

Your father wanted a villain.
He chose the wrong person.

"Your grandfather is not a good man. Yes, Sam was living a life that was wrong for him, but he would never have cheated. And he loved your father and would never have left him."

"Pamela and your grandfather were together long before the divorce. Sam pretended not to see."

"But Pamela told him Sam's secret, about the cross-dressing and feeling stuck in the wrong body...Your grandfather took it as some huge insult, and he lost control."

"Sam wound up in the emergency room."

He said if he ever came back, he'd do the same to your father.
Sam was terrified. Was never even allowed to say goodbye.
It broke his heart.

I...I...had no idea...
Sam kept that secret to the grave. But Sam's gone, and I'm not keeping secrets anymore.

"We met months after all that."

When did you know?
When did I know what?
That you were...you know... a lesbian.

Oh, I'm not a lesbian.
DINA

Everybody has a natural preference. I happened to be a sucker for a man in uniform...

...and Sam looked damn good in a suit.

We don't get to choose who we love. But sometimes you get lucky and fall for someone wonderful.

Did you know Sam became a lawyer? Specialized in domestic violence cases.
Wow.

He organized marches in Washington. We helped found a foster care organization for transgender teens thrown out of their homes. Sam was so smart, and kind, and...

Ha. Listen to me. I'm as bad as your father. Everyone's memory of the past is imperfect, and mine is, too, because I can't remember any of Sam's flaws!

Wait! Board games. I hated playing board games with him! He always won! With huge rows of hotels in Monopoly. And he would smile the whole time, the jerk!

And there were other days...

"...I'd find him staring at a wall. I couldn't talk to him. I could barely look at him. You could see the pain, you could see how much he missed your father. And how much he loved you."
"Sam never got to tell you how much."

sniff
sniff

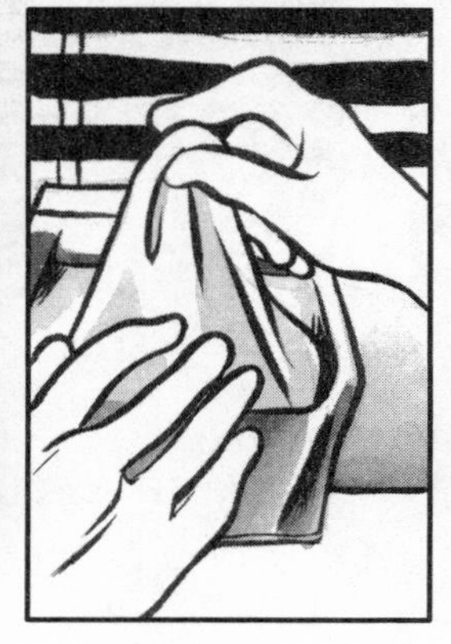

It breaks my heart that I'll never get to know Sam Orham. But if Dina was any proof...

...he was a pretty amazing guy.

I finally decided on my one frivolous thing: an old Volvo built like a tank. A tank that could handle my driving and the occasional small run-in with a stationary object until I got better.

I'd like to say I was happy, that I didn't miss Cat, Adam, and Laura like crazy.

Maybe I'll still say it.

But I still went to church every Sunday with Mom. If she was secretly praying for me to be "cured," she never let on.

Me, I just prayed for God to tell my mom that it's okay. Weirdly enough, church was one of the only places I FELT okay.

It reminded me that not all people were horrible.

This seat free?

Cheese fries?

I figured I owe you a few.

Um... Mads, you got a little something on your face.

The rally starts at ten and it'll take us about four hours to drive there.
I don't want to do math.
No whining allowed. You knew the requirements when you took the job of VP.
GSA TODAY

Speaking of which, Amanda, do you mind wearing black sunglasses and a Secret Service earpiece?
I mean, what's the sense of being in office if I can't do it in style?
Haha.

Shades are fine, but you are NOT allowed to take a bullet for this guy.
Awww, so sweet.
I'm not being sweet. I've just seen you play Whac-A-Mole. Reflexes: not your strong suit.

Whatever. I still beat you at SkeeBall!
You did not! Those tickets came from the kid before you!

What?! Oh, it's ON.
Get a room, you two.

Uh. I gotta go, see you tomorrow at... *sigh* six a.m.

Everyone at school knew me before I was me. Let's just say they weren't the most understanding. But at the Zipper, no one questioned who I was.

I'm sure the assholes are going to tell you and I'd rather you hear it from me—

RESIST THE CIS-TEM
GAY IS GOOD
NO HATE
GAY IS THE NEW BLACK
What'd you write?

"Let My Little Brother Get Married So Someone Else Will Have to Deal with His Whiny Shit" didn't fit.
CIVIL RIGHTS FOR EVERYONE
Ugh. I have no idea what to write! How do you sum up your whole system of beliefs with a dollar-store poster?!
I can't believe you are eating ketchup chips this early in the morning.
Not eating. Drinking. Too tired to chew.

Stop being gross and help me.
One step ahead of you.

R.I.P. SAM ORHAM,
TRANSGENDER
LAWYER IN NY STATE:
PIONEER, ADVOCATE,
USBAND, HERO

Being amazing seems to run in your family.

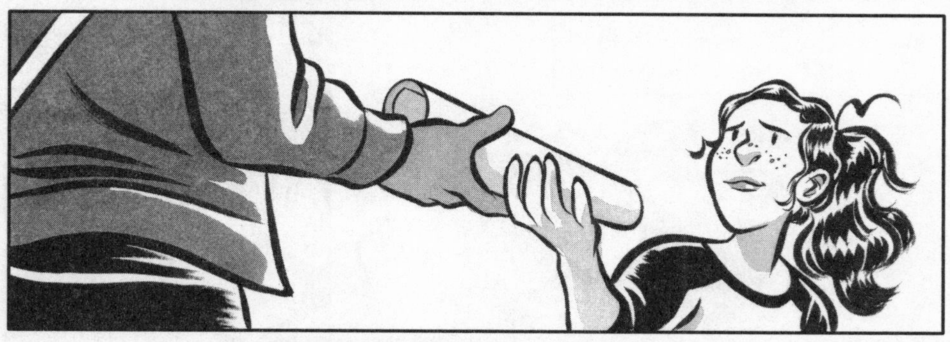

KISS NUMBER 9

Kiss Number 9 was over before I realized what I was doing.
Kiss Number 9 tasted like ketchup chips.

(Seriously, who eats ketchup chips?!)

And Kiss Number 9...

Um...what was I saying?

HA HA

GAY PRIDE
FIGHT FOR
WE WANT
PROTECT TRANS TROOPS
Kinda crazy that I had ever thought I was alone.
R.I.P. SAM ORKHAM, TRANSGENDER LAWYER IN NY STATE: PIONEER, ADVOCATE, HUSBAND, HERO

Hmmm.

SWITCH!

Are you sure you're ready?
How many seasons is it?

Enough to last well beyond tomorrow!
All right... Bring it on.
Woo!

EPISODE ONE OF VALLEY OF THE HIDDEN: "CANOE TELL ME THE WAY TO SAN JOSE"
Wooooo!

Seven hours later.
I think my butt fell off.
I'd help you look for it but I forgot how to make my legs move. Legs! Move!
Noooooooo. But she was dead!
They all saw her get mauled by the cheetahs!
How can she still be alive?!

NEXT EPISODE OF VALLEY OF THE HIDDEN: "CHEETAHING DEATH"
Honey, it's time to call it a day.
But there are only eleven more episodes! We can do it! Amanda, you with me?!

Amanda's not here right now, please leave a message.
What are you going to do when you have to wait months for a new episode?
Hmmm... good point.

This was really fun.
Thanks. Not just for tonight. I missed both of you...
...and, you know...I'm okay with...you know.

Legs! MOVE!

Hey, it worked that time! Good night.
Wait!

Your mom didn't abandon you. Grandpa made him leave, threatened to hurt you if he didn't disappear. Told you he was crazy and cheating on him. Nothing ever happened with Dina and Sam until well after.

They lied to you, just like you all lied to me. And Sam...my REAL grandparent, spent the rest of his life missing you.
But you would never give him a chance.

Please... Please just come out to dinner with Dina. Do it for me. Please.

Okay. I'll do it.
You promise?

For you, yes, I promise.

So Dad arrived. Dina and he got along amazingly. They're even talking about forming a bowling team.

Oh, and Grandma and Grandpa Orham joined us as well. Grandpa must have apologized for three hours. It was really moving.

We ate with Laura and her new girlfriend, with Adam and Cat, and Father Tim and sweet Sara Miller. Jess and Nate's band played on the jukebox, since they had gotten pretty big by this point. Also, I finally got a superpower. Laser beams from my eyes. I would have done a demonstration, but I didn't want anyone to get jealous and ruin such a perfect evening.

Or, you know, maybe, just maybe, despite the fact he never breaks his promises, despite the fact he knew how much this meant to me...

...my dad just didn't show.
SAM ORHAM,
TRANSGENDER
LAWYER IN NY STATE:
PIONEER, ADVOCATE,
HUSBAND, HERO

Mads, I just—

DRAGONS AND DAGGERS!
PLAYER 1, VILLAGERS SELECTED.

PLAYER 2, CHOOSE YOUR DRAGON.

KISS NUMBER 8
LAURA

KISS NUMBER 9
NATE

KISS NUMBER 10
KELLY

KISS NUMBER 11
JOHANNA

KISS NUMBER 12
LUCAS

KISS NUMBER 13
MARIA

KISS NUMBER 14
ZOEY

ZOEY

AND LITTLE SAM

Tornado

Q&A

with Author Colleen AF Venable
and Artist Ellen T. Crenshaw

Colleen: What was your first kiss?

E: I was a freshman in college before I had my first kiss! He was an RA for my dorm network, so we were very secretive (or at least we thought we were—of course we weren't AT ALL stealthy). It was in his dorm room, he was a perfect gentleman, and it was a very good kiss!

C: Aw. My first was with my pillow, and if you ask me, that pillow needed a LOT of pointers. Luckily my first kiss with a HUMAN (now my kissing preference) was a lot better. I was fourteen and hanging upside down in the playground. My boyfriend of three months Spider-Manned me with a lovely sweet, short kiss.

E: He Spider-Manned you before Spider-Manning was even a thing??!?
Dang, that's romantic!

Colleen: What was your worst kiss?

E: Okay, so maybe my first kiss was in high school, but I don't like to count it because I wasn't a willing participant. Senior year, a friend confessed his feelings for me in a note in my yearbook, and at our graduation he planted a big wet one on me and scampered away. I don't remember if we ever spoke again.

C: Nope. Definitely doesn't count. Let me guess, he's a "nice guy" who is always stuck in "the friend zone"? Excuse me while I scream into my old pillow boyfriend.

Colleen: If you could give any advice to your sixteen-year-old self, what would it be?

E: I think if I could give sixteen-year-old me advice, it would actually be to get in more trouble. And not to worry so much. I was a very uptight kid—much like Laura! Good to a fault. I don't regret being a goody-goody, but I could have spared myself some anguish by loosening up a little. (I could've had more kisses!)

C: What?! I don't believe this. You're too cool to have been a goody-goody. Are you just covering up your Buffy-style vampire-killing spree?
The advice I'd give myself is "Don't put your head in that half-solidified Jell-O vodka bowl. Yes, you'll win five dollars on the bet, BUT it will also dye your face red FOR A WEEK." Also "Don't starve yourself."

E: Colleen, you would've been the Buffy to my Willow. I would've taken you to TGIFriday's in the Grey Goblin (my car, an '88 Honda Accord—which, fun fact, is also Laura's car) and we would've shared a brownie sundae.

Ellen: Describe your high school best friend.

C: My middle school best friend, Brandy, moved back to Texas in eighth grade. She was super creative, wildly goofy, and brilliant. When high school started I became the sort of person who had lots of close friends but no real best friend. I jumped from social groups easily and didn't quite let anyone get to know me all that well (...or else they might notice I only ate two slices of fat-free bologna a day. Seriously, sixteen-year-old Colleen, stop that!). I focused on schoolwork, art, and making out with anything that moved. I dated a LOT in high school.

E: Aw, sweet Colleen! My high school BFF was Shanon (with one *n*). We went to elementary, middle, and high school together. She was a lot cooler and more popular at school than I was, but she never made me feel like I wasn't cool. Art connected us, and she introduced me to music that wasn't my mom's oldies cassettes or Disney musicals (which are still awesome, but that's all I knew!). We're still friends to this day, but she's not my BFF—she's my family.

C: Okay, that just made me tear up. If this was an episode of *Full House*, the music would totally be playing.

Ellen: What was your favorite band/musician in high school?

C: I was super into punk, but the nerdier side of it, like Atom & His Package, and Me First & The Gimme Gimmes. I listened to a TON of Beatles, and mystery mix tapes from friends who were too lazy to label them, and my love of witty lyrics made me fall for Barenaked Ladies, Bloodhound Gang, and Weird Al. I feel no shame! One of those three is still in my regular listening rotation.

E: I hope it's Weird Al.

C: "Another One Rides the Bus" 4 Eva!

Ellen: Tell me about your first high school rock show!!!

C: Went on a date to see Third Eye Blind at the Chance (woot-woot Hudson Valley, NY). They were okay, but the opening band was so weird and lovely it kinda blew my mind. They were called Thin Lizard Dawn because only three-word bands were allowed in the '90s, it seems. I accidentally crowd-surfed. It was an amazing night and made me realize there were a whole bunch of "pay $5 to see a buttload of weird bands you've never heard of" shows.

E: Third Eye Blind was your first show?! Get OUT of here. Mine was Jars of Clay at a local Christian community college. But I did get to see Third Eye Blind years later, headlining with Goo Goo Dolls, opened by Live. (To solidify this as the most '90s statement ever, I also feel it's important to mention that I got swept up in the short-lived swing music craze—no regrets!)

Ellen: With whom in *KN8* do you relate the most?

C: Personality-wise and in terms of making bad decisions, I'm very Amanda. In terms of sexuality, I'm totally a Dina—not into defining myself, with a preference for fellas or very masculine ladies (Hello, JD from Le Tigre). In my mind Dina didn't think twice about falling in love with Sam. If the right person comes along, no matter who they are, I'd like to think I wouldn't either. Also, I could live in diners.

Ellen: When I designed the look of the characters, I definitely drew on people from real life (no pun intended).

C: I drew on people, too, but it was just that one sleepover. I'm sorry, Kim's older brother!

Ellen: Did you base any characters on people in real life? Was anyone in particular a big influence?

C: The only character who came directly from real life was Franco. I actually love minor-league baseball, but mostly for the hot dog costume races and people like Franco: guys over their prime but still doing what they love. The real Franco played for the Pittsfield Mets from Massachusetts. I worked in Pittsfield one summer and eventually decided I didn't care who won as long as Franco got a home run. Most of the other characters were conglomerations of people I knew, but Mr. Orham was definitely influenced by Keith Mars. I was watching *Veronica Mars* mid-first draft and the quick back and forths of father-daughter goofiness made me so happy.

E: Oh my God, I based Mr. Orham's design on Mike O'Malley as Kurt's dad on *Glee*. Very similar physical type to Keith Mars.

Colleen: So funny! Who else did you model the characters after?

E: Some folks are based on actors—Grandma and Grandpa Orham are based on Helen Mirren and Spencer Tracy, respectively—

C: Helen Mirren! THAT would explain why I have a crush on Grandma Orham.

E: —but most of the character designs are based on people I know. This is not the first time I secretly raided friends' Facebook photos for reference. For instance, many of Cat's details—her black fingernails, bracelets, eye makeup, thumbhole sweater, and that sweet checkered belt—are based on the aforementioned BFF, Shanon.

C: Shanon just got even cooler in my mind. Um...can I be friends with her, too?!

Ellen: What inspired you to begin writing this story?

C: My older sister coming out in our very, very Catholic family. Suddenly I went from the bad kid (reminder: Jell-O vodka face) to the good kid just because I went on dates with guys. The other thing was that I started writing *Kiss* in 2004 and at that time the number of YA works that had any trans characters I could count on one hand. Hell, I probably only needed one finger! (*Luna* by Julie Anne Peters came out in 2004.) I wanted to write something for the teens trying to figure out who they were. And while I'm not religious anymore, I wanted to write a story of coming out where religion wasn't the bad guy. (I've got two amazing aunts who are nuns and they are the most caring, welcoming humans on Earth.) Also in 2004 there was a lot of backlash online for anyone who had come out as gay, but then realized they were bi. One web cartoonist in particular received such unkindness that I decided I wanted Amanda to not just come out of the closet, but I wanted her to keep exploring all sides of her sexuality once she was out.

C: How long did it take you to draw *Kiss*?

E: Just under two years. But I know the book had quite a history before I was attached to it. How long did it take you to write?

C: It took me three years of writing...then six months of submitting to publishers/peeing my pants with every email, then... Let's just say graphic novels take a LONG time to make.

E: Preach!

C: *Kiss* went from being a contemporary novel to a period piece, but I think it is more timeless that way. 2004 was a crazy rough time to come out as queer. Gay marriage wasn't even legal in 2004! It feels like a century ago... We've come a long way, baby! Wait, that's a cigarette slogan? Can we claim it back? "We've come a long way, don't-call-me-baby." There. Much better.

E: I actually love that this book has become a time capsule. There's internet, but smart-phones were not common. AOL Instant Messager was the rage. It was equally likely that a person could have a portable cassette player, CD player, or MP3 player. It's like a major transition period: politically, socially, and technologically. There's a specificity to how the teens in *Kiss* communicate–Mads uses IMs and texts with Cat and Laura, but calls her grandparents on the landline and encounters their answering machine. Mr. Orham can take away Mads's computer and cell phone and not render her completely unable to do her homework.

C: I was even tempted to give Mads her own LiveJournal. R.I.P LiveJournal days.

E: I think the fact that she MOST DEFINITELY has a LiveJournal is implied.

Ellen: What is your writing process?

C: It's a three-step process: Hang out in loud places. Giggle at my own jokes. Eat pie. I'm a big believer in only writing a few days a week...though those other days I'm working out the story in my mind so when I finally sit at a computer, words just fall out of my fingers. If I sat staring at a blank screen every single day I think I would get discouraged. Also, maybe a human shouldn't eat that much pie every day. Maaaybe.

Ellen: What is it like, as a writer, to have your story interpreted and conveyed by another artist? Is there anything in particular that turned out differently than you imagined?

C: It is 100 percent the greatest thing! I get so so giddy about collaboration that it's hard for me to do anything other than squeal when I see your artwork. Little things, but mostly jokes that I wrote that were only half working until you made them work!

E: Aw, shucks!

C: And character designs: I'm not even sure how I imagined Nate, but as soon as I saw your drawing of him, I was like, *THAT'S NATE*. Those ears! I would have swooned super hard on him in high school.

Colleen: If you were sixteen again, which character in *KN8* would you have a crush on?

E: I mean, Nate, obviously! There's a reason he's designed like that! He's basically an amalgam of every boy I ever crushed on.

C: I'd love to think I would have chosen Nate, but sadly I think I would have been all about K. I liked the moody punks. Just ask my mom about the guy with the dog collar and foot- long green Mohawk. She loved him!

E: To be fair, I think the whole Zipper crowd is worth crushing on.

Ellen: Describe your typical weekend outfit when you were sixteen. (You wore uniforms to Catholic school, yes?)

C: Actually I lucked out, and despite being super Catholic, the only Catholic school by me was insanely tiny with a not-so-great rep. SO I went to Valley Central (not to be confused with Bayside's bulldog rivals) and covered myself in a LOT of neon and vintage, mostly stuff my mom wore in the '70s that I found and stole from our attic. My favorite outfit was a pair of red plaid pants with a pink mesh half shirt. Yes, HALF shirt. I am thankful there is no photographic evidence of this.

E: I, however, am extremely sad there are no photos! It sounds like you were the baddest babe on the block! I wore boys' camp shirts from Goodwill and cargo pants, plus these black Skechers that looked like they were from the Mickey Mouse oeuvre.

Ellen: Who was your favorite fictional character when you were sixteen? (Or who was your biggest crush?)

C: I had the major hots for Pavel Bure, the Russian Rocket, who played for the Vancouver Canucks. I wasn't into hockey until I saw him—such a graceful skater with blue eyes that could melt the rink—and my hormones were like, "YOU ARE SO INTO HOCKEY NOW." Because the internet was still a baby, the only way I got pics of him to drool on was to take photos of the TV during live games. Like real photos. With film. Because I am two thousand years old.

You?

E: I don't mean to make so many *Buffy the Vampire Slayer* references, but Angel, hands down. Of course, nowadays I question the motives of a 241-year-old vampire in love with a sixteen-year-old girl, but at the time it was SO DREAMY.

C: You are so right! I remember friends crushing on Giles and me thinking, "Ew, he's an old man," but he was like two hundred years younger than Angel!

Colleen: What did your locker look like in high school?

E: I never had one of those tall lockers. At my school they were three rows high, and mine was at the bottom. I was too concerned with getting trampled to decorate it. You?

C: Someone once described my college dorm with my friend Jodie as looking like "an Applebee's threw-up all over our walls." My HS locker was the same way. Every single inch was covered in something, from Far Side comics, to cute stickers, to handwritten super-inspirational quotes like "Get high on milk because the cows are on grass!" and "Bad Spellers of the World Untie!"

E: I'm beginning to understand where Mr. Orham's excellent dad puns come from.

C: Those are in my DNA. Poppa V is the king of puns.

Colleen: I can't get over how amazingly you draw angsty teen body language. How did you get such great poses?

E: I take a ton of self-reference photos. Body language is my favorite, and I always try to say as much as I can with a pose. I'll even act it out sometimes if I need a little help figuring out the emotions in a scene.

Colleen: What's the hardest thing about interpreting a script?

E: My main goal in interpreting a script is achieving the right pacing and emotional beats, staying true to the author's vision while not sacrificing my own. If the script is well written, like *Kiss*, it's easy to translate it to the page. At worst I struggled making dialogue-heavy scenes fit, but page design is a fun problem to solve. The hard part is maintaining stamina when you've got over three hundred pages to draw! I've been making comics for decades, but this was my first graphic novel. It was like learning how to run a marathon while in the middle of a race.

C: I still can't believe this is your first book. The whole collaboration process was amazing! I'm totally going to get a T-shirt made that says "I got to work with Ellen Crenshaw first." Please remember me when you are working with...um...the most famous person I can think of is the Pope? Haha, damn you, Catholic roots!

E: It was a truly unique and wonderful collaboration experience with you. And it's not our first collab! We did a one-shot comic together about turning the tables on a subway creeper. It's how I knew we'd work well together on a big project.

Colleen: What advice would you give to aspiring graphic novel artists?

E: Estimate how long something is going to take you, and then triple it. Take lots of breaks! The suffering-artist trope is for the birds. Prioritize your health and well-being.

C: So true. We should do another book for teens that's just that last line four thousand times in a row.

Colleen: Art nerd time! What tools did you use to draw *KN8*?

E: I penciled the book in Photoshop using my trusty old Wacom Intuos4. Then I printed the pages in blue line onto Arches hot press watercolor paper. (My printer is an Epson R1900. You may note that my equipment is a few generations old, because I hate updating when something works.) I inked the pages with Dr. Ph. Martin's Black Star HiCarb ink and Winsor & Newton Series 7 brushes. (Many brushes died in the making of this book.) The tones were done with the same ink and a variety of synthetic watercolor brushes. Then I scanned each page with my Epson V500 scanner. Whew!

Colleen: The Tornadoes were inspired by my fave minor-league team, the Coney Island Cyclones. I like to pretend Coney Island is my backyard since it's only fifteen minutes from where I live, and I looooove the part where they dress people up in giant hot dog costumes with varying condiments and make them race across the field. Super-important question: Who wins: ketchup, relish, or mustard?

E: Mustard, Colleen. Mustard.

C: Buuuut if you cheer for ketchup and it's not winning, you get to yell "CATCH-UP, KETCHUP!" Eh? Eh? Get it? Okay...I'll see myself out.

E: Yeah, but when ketchup loses, you can say they didn't cut the mustard.

For Kath, the strongest person I've ever known.
—COLLEEN

For my family, without whom I
could not do what I do, or be what I am.
—ELLEN

Published by First Second
First Second is an imprint of Roaring Brook Press, a division of
Holtzbrinck Publishing Holdings Limited Partnership
175 Fifth Avenue, New York, NY 10010

Library of Congress Control Number: 2018938071

Paperback ISBN: 978-1-59643-709-8
Hardcover ISBN: 978-1-250-19693-4

First edition, 2019

Edited by Calista Brill and Aimee Fleck
Book design by Dezi Sienty and Molly Johanson

Penciled in Photoshop with Frenden's blue pencil. Inked and toned on Arches 140 lb. hot press
watercolor paper, with Dr. Ph. Martin's Black Star HiCarb ink and Winsor & Newton Series 7 brushes.

Printed in the United States of America
Paperback: 10 9 8 7 6 5 4 3 2 1
Hardcover: 10 9 8 7 6 5 4 3 2 1